Dreams are precious things. T 
silver, yet they are free. They
each one is unique. They live
situation and can always be big, no matter ...
feel. They are like a candle in a dark room; they light the way
ahead.

Everyone can own a dream, no matter who they are or
where they are from. Dreams must be loved, treasured,
nurtured and encouraged in order to grow strong and blossom.
Sometimes dreams have to rest for a while. Sometimes they
gather dust. Sometimes they take you on unexpected journeys
and far away from where you thought you would be.
Sometimes it's easy and sometimes it's hard. But whatever
happens, they must never be thrown away.

Ernie Gonzales
The determined dreamer

Written by Beth Shepherd
Illustrated by Lisa Buckridge

An icy prison

Ernie lay in shock. He had fallen, splat, onto a rotten soggy avocado and had sunk down inside. All that could be seen of him were his tentacles and his boggly eyes poking out from the green mush. He had given up trying to wriggle free; after all, his dream was well and truly over. He had proven everyone right – he was a daydreamer. And now he was a failed daydreamer.

It was Thursday, which was market day in the small Spanish village of Vinuella. The heat of the summer sun was blazing as a man carried a heavy box of vegetables back from the market. Ernie lay inside the box feeling sorry for himself and munching on the green avocado mush. Outside he could

5

hear a lot of banging and door shutting and then, with one last slam of a door, everything went deadly silent and darkness fell upon him. As he lay there in the stillness, surrounded by the warmth of the avocado, he suddenly noticed that his tentacles felt strangely cold. Despite feeling that his life had ended, he couldn't help wondering what was going on around him. Intrigued, he wriggled out of the avocado and landed on a cool cucumber. He looked around but all he could see was a thick blanket of darkness. His heart began to race; he had no idea where he was. He felt confused, alone and afraid. As the darkness pressed in around his tiny shell, he felt the temperature dropping rapidly. His slimy body began to shiver and he noticed that his tentacles were beginning to stiffen, and his lips were turning blue. In a state of panic he tried to escape, but his suction slime had turned to ice and he felt himself beginning to slide down the cucumber into the depths of the box.

Desperately he fumbled around in the darkness, looking for something to hold on to. He was almost at the bottom of the box when he finally managed to wrap his stiff tentacles around the stalk of an apple. Ernie breathed a sigh of relief. As he swung in the air in the cold darkness it dawned on him that this could be his last moment on earth. But just then he heard a noise; it seemed to be footsteps coming towards him. Ernie was terrified! He had to hide in case they, whoever they were, were coming for him. Quickly he began to swing from side to side, gaining speed until eventually he managed to grab hold of the leaves on the top of a carrot. As he scrambled to pull himself under them, he somehow dislodged a large turnip. With a thud it dropped down and hit the end of the carrot, flipping Ernie high up in the air and out of the vegetable box. SMACK! He felt himself hit the top of what seemed to be a large, cold, metal box. With speed he came plummeting back down. Splodge! He landed on the soggy avocado once again.

The footsteps came to a halt, right outside the metal box. Ernie heard the sound of a door opening and suddenly a dazzlingly bright light broke through the darkness. In an instant the whole of the new world he had found himself in was lit up. For a moment or two he was blinded by the light and the avocado mush. 'This must be the doorway to heaven,' he mumbled, wiping his eyes and climbing out of the avocado to explore this strange snail heaven. However, what he saw in front of him made him jump right out of his shell. Two huge human faces towered above him. They had opened the front of the cold, metal box and were now looking straight at him.

Ernie felt the warmth coming back to his body and his tentacles beginning to defrost. 'Phew! I am not dying,' he said. 'I must be in someone's fridge!' Then, before he had time to work out what was going on, a large hand came straight towards him. Everything went black as he passed out and slid down the side of the cucumber.

Dreams of the Olive Garden

When Ernie came round he discovered that he was in what seemed to be a ready-made snail home on the window sill in someone's kitchen.

A whole week had passed since that dreadful day, and Ernie was feeling very scared and alone. As he sat next to the window he began to go over the events of last Thursday, trying once again to make sense of it all.

The day had started like any other, with the smell of his Mama's cooking filling the house. Ernie awoke unusually early and as he lay in bed he noticed a strange stirring in his heart. It was something he had not felt before. He had a strong

feeling that it was time to set off on a journey to reach his dreams: the Olive Garden. Eagerly he jumped out of bed, stretched his tentacles and took a long yawn. Then he pulled out a box from his cupboard that was labelled 'STUFF FOR MY ADVENTURE' in big, bold letters. Inside it he had packed everything for this daring journey, including a large sketch pad with a series of drawings and maps entitled 'My Cunning Plan'. There was also a lot of random stuff that he had no idea whether he would need: a large blob of pink chewed chewing gum, a small yo-yo, a small mint with a hole in the middle and a cotton bud. Feeling satisfied with his chosen items, he confidently threw all the contents from the dusty box into his rucksack.

For as long as he could remember, Ernie had been dreaming of finding this elusive 'Olive Garden'; it was said to be snail paradise. As a small snail he was raised on stories of this wonderful place. He would sit for hours listening to his grandfather Manuel, or Papa as Ernie fondly called him, tell him about row after row of lush, green cabbages, shaded by beautiful olive trees, with endless delicious, succulent olives lining the floor for snails to feast upon. There was said to be a pool at the end of the garden which was the most luxurious pool any snail had ever set eyes upon. Surrounding the beautiful, warm pool were sweet-smelling lemon trees, and every afternoon a gentle breeze blew a few leaves down from the trees into the water. Ernie would imagine jumping onto a leaf and sailing across the pool to Lemon Harbour, the wind blowing through his tentacles, and spending the evening

relaxing and sipping honey nectar. Ernie was dazzled by his Papa's stories. Night after night he would beg him to tell them all over again.

His Papa was the great-great-grandson of a travelling family of snails. One day, many years ago, they passed through the village telling stories of a paradise garden. With passion they told the villagers about this amazing place. They encouraged them to come back with them to start a new and better life in the garden, but not a single snail in the village believed their story – in fact, they just laughed at them. The visitors tried to return to the garden but the river had dried up, and that was the only way to get there. Forced to stay, they built their lives there in the village, ignored and ridiculed by everyone. Ernie's family were no different to the rest. And, although the legend still remained, it was forbidden in his family to talk about it because of the shame it would bring on them from the rest of the village.

However, Papa chose to believe the legend. Long ago, when he was a young snail, he had tried to escape to find it, but his family found out and they were so angry with him they made him promise to never do it again. So Manuel stayed in the village, but he enjoyed telling his favourite grandson Ernie all the stories that had been passed on to him by his ancestors and which he still treasured in his heart.

Ernie was one of a large family of snails, the Gonzales. They were well known for the vegetable paella his Mama made. Snails from all over the village would sit outside his house waiting for a plateful of this delicious Spanish dish. He had five sisters and five brothers, and Ernie was slap-bang in the middle. Life in his family was chaotic, loud and eventful. There was always a drama of some kind going on: if it was not his eldest brother Paulo getting into trouble for spending the whole night leaf surfing down the hill, then it was the whole family having to go and rescue his youngest sister who had been caught in a piece of chewing gum on her way home from school.

The family home was a plant pot next to a house on the main road running through Vinuella. It was dark and dusty and they lived with the constant smell of fumes from passing cars and the fear of being stepped upon. None of his family, apart from Papa, had ever seen grass or trees or even eaten fresh food, and they lived on vegetable peelings that fell  from the kitchen window of the house above them. In short, life was gloomy, and ever since his eldest sister had been found squashed on the pavement, life at home had become even more miserable.

Ernie had spent his childhood dreaming of the Olive Garden and planning his adventure to get there. Patiently he waited for the time to come for him to leave and to start his brave journey. Then one day his Papa told him excitedly that the river had finally started to flow again. So that evening during dinner he climbed up onto the table and courageously announced to his family that he was going to lead them all there, promising them a better life with lots of land, space and fresh food, and that there would be no chance of anyone else ever being stepped on.

There was a moment of silence before his brothers burst out laughing and the rest of his family told him to get off the table and to never mention the stupid idea ever again. From then on he just stayed quietly in his room as the chaos continued around him. No one ever seemed to take any notice of him, and life at home became busier and gloomier. Ernie just couldn't stand being there. He dreamed of peace and quiet, somewhere he could call his own. He didn't think he would be missed if he left, as the only one who ever seemed to take any notice of him was Papa. So he decided to leave and make a new life for himself in the Olive Garden. No one had ever dared to believe his Papa's amazing story except him, and now the time had come for him to prove them wrong and to follow his grandfather's dream.

Excited and ready to let his journey unfold, Ernie hoisted the heavy rucksack onto his back with his long tentacles, grabbed some cabbage leaves and quietly slipped out of the house, shutting the door behind him.

A cunning plan

With his overloaded rucksack on his back, Ernie sat on the
steps near his house and waited, his shell straining under the
weight. He was confident, and knew without a doubt that he
would make it to the Olive Garden – he just had no idea how.
All he knew for certain was that he needed to get to the river
at the bottom of the hill. As he watched the sun rise over the
housetops he waited for an idea to come to him. But his mind
was blank. An hour passed and still nothing. He pulled his

sketch pad from his bag and began to doodle ideas. He was so
deep in thought that he didn't notice a large pair of boots
marching straight towards him. With one last step they
slammed down beside him. Ernie almost jumped out of his
shell!

13

Dazed, he looked around, and to his shock he realised that he was now millimetres away from being squashed. Nervously he stretched his long neck up towards the sky and there, towering above him, was a very large man. The slightest move from him and Ernie would be as flat as a pancake. His heart pounded with terror. Then without thinking he grabbed his sketch pad and with all his strength slid away as fast as he could. Seconds later a dark shadow appeared above his head, blocking out the morning sun. Puzzled, Ernie looked up and gasped. Then he dived forward, slipped inside his shell and rolled along the cobbled floor, just as a large cardboard box came crashing down behind him, sending him flying high into the air.

Ernie's heart was pounding. Inside his shell it sounded as loud as a drum. He took a deep breath and poked his small head out to see what had happened. There beside him was a large box of vegetables. His mind raced as he tried desperately to think what to do next. But before he had time to decide he heard a loud knocking as the vegetable man banged on the door above him. A few seconds later he heard the sound of a woman's voice as the door creaked open. 'Hola, buenos dias,' said the man as he greeted her. Ernie shuddered; being this close to humans was just not wise. 'I have to get out of here,' he said to himself, beginning to panic. 'It's not safe.' But just as he began sliding away from the box, an idea came to him. 'That's it!' he shouted with excitement. 'That veggie box is the best way to the river!' Bravely he turned back and slid and slooched along the ground to the box as fast as he could. Anxiously he listened as the humans talked above him, and the tiny hairs on his head stood on end. Once the woman

14

had paid the man for her vegetables Ernie knew he had only a few seconds before the box was lifted up and carried to the next house.

He was almost there when the woman shut the door. Immediately the vegetable man bent down, and once again the large shadow descended on Ernie's world. It was now or never. With one last push he slid up the side of the brown cardboard box, clinging on with his best suction slime, just as it left the ground. His adventure had begun.

The Fiesta

Ernie wobbled as the man lifted the heavy box off the ground. Rapidly the floor moved further and further away from him as the man lifted the box high up on his shoulders. The ground seemed so far away that Ernie was sure he must almost be in the clouds. Sticking vertically to the side of the box was exhausting, and Ernie knew that he had to get inside it to safety before his suction ran out of power.

As the man continued his rounds up the hill, stopping at each door on his way, Ernie slid up and over the side of the box and fell in amongst the vegetables. Patiently he waited for the man to head down to the river. But it seemed to take forever and Ernie was sure that before long he would be squashed between two very large beetroots. He was hoping that the man would throw any unsold vegetables over the wall onto the giant compost heap which was just next to the river. Then all he would need to do would be to find a way to sail downstream to his beloved garden. However, the veggies in the box didn't seem to be going down, which meant they were not selling.

'Why is no one buying anything?' Ernie heard the man mumble. He sounded frustrated. 'What's going on?' wondered Ernie, as he used his best snail suction power to pull himself away from the beetroots. 'Where is everyone?' Suddenly he heard a noise; the air seemed to be full of laughter and music. Cautiously he stretched up his long neck so that he could see over the top of the box, but it was no good – he was too small. Looking around, he found a hole big enough to pop his head through. He gasped.

16

It looked as if the man was taking the unsold vegetables back down the hill towards the vegetable market, and towards the music. He was beginning to feel a little sick as the box crashed up and down as the man stomped grumpily along the road. 'This was not part of my plan,' Ernie said to himself as he struggled to keep his balance. He had already lost his rucksack somewhere amongst the radishes.

When the man finally stopped, Ernie held his breath. To his amazement, stretched out in front of him lay the river in full flow. 'Yes!' he shouted in delight, bracing himself to be thrown over the wall. However, no sooner had the man stopped than he was off again. 'STOP!!' Ernie yelled at the top of his lungs. 'You're going the wrong way!' Ernie could hear the sound of stones crunching under the man's feet as the river disappeared out of view. He wondered if they were now in the park.

Just as Ernie was beginning to get his bearings, he heard the familiar voice boom above his head. 'Couldn't sell anything this morning,' said the vegetable man. 'Everyone must be here at the Fiesta.' Ernie was puzzled. 'I'll leave this box at your stall. Maybe you'll have a better chance of selling them.' CRASH!! The man slammed the box down on the table, sending Ernie flying high in the air along with the vegetables.

As he spun through the sky with a few onions, Ernie looked around the park and saw a big banner for 'The Annual Summer Fiesta'. 'Oh no! Of course, today is the annual summer Fiesta. How could I have forgotten?' he said, feeling annoyed with himself. Just before he came plummeting back down into the box he caught a brief glimpse of people dancing in brightly coloured flamenco dresses and tucking into Spanish paella. 'What a bad day to pick to start my journey,' he said, feeling deflated as he slid down the side of a carrot. 'Great! My fantastic journey has amounted to nothing more than a close encounter with a beetroot.' He wondered how this day could have gone so wrong.

Ernie thought about making a quick dash for it. Maybe he could slide up over the edge of the box and carefully slip out of the park, but the idea of sliding across rough gravel stones made him shudder and his tentacles frizzle. And besides, there were so many people dancing he was bound to end up stuck to the bottom of someone's shoe. Desperate to find another way of escaping, he cautiously poked his head out of the hole again. Immediately he felt the blazing hot sun on his tiny green head. 'Wow, today is a real scorcher!' It was so hot that he was sure he would fry in his shell if he left the shady box, so gloomily he slid back down amongst the cool vegetables. Just as he was getting out his sketch pad and beginning to draw up an escape plan, he heard the sound of people approaching the stall. There were voices, followed by a rustling sound and, before he knew it, Ernie and the vegetables had been sold!

He felt the box being lifted up once again. Frantically he squirmed to get away from the heavy vegetables that were wobbling dangerously next to him. 'I have to find a way to escape!' he shouted to himself. Then, to his relief, he spotted his rucksack. Quickly he grabbed it and flung it onto his back. Then, with all the strength he could muster, he made his way to the top of the box. However, just as he was about to peek his boggly eyes over the rim to see what was happening, the weight of his overloaded rucksack pulled him back into the box and he landed, splat, in the soggy avocado.

The determined dreamer

Even though it had been a week since Ernie had found himself in the avocado in the vegetable box inside the fridge, the events of last Thursday still haunted him. Since coming to after passing out, he had been living on the window sill in someone's kitchen, in what seemed to be a ready-made snail home. He had no idea where the kitchen was or why he was there. In short, he was well and truly baffled. Bright sunlight broke through the clouds, interrupting his thoughts. As he stared longingly at the beautiful Spanish mountains, the blue sky and the sunshine, it dawned on him just how trapped he really was. It had been ages since he had breathed fresh air or felt the sun on his green slimy skin. It felt like a lifetime since he had spoken to another snail, and the loneliness was beginning to get to him. He pressed his nose up against the glass and let out a long sigh, causing it to steam up.

In his strange new 'home', Ernie seemed to have everything he needed, as well as a lot of wonderful things that he didn't even know he needed. His house was strangely perfect: just the right size for a snail, and warm and cosy. Inside was a snug sofa and a bookshelf full of delightful snail stories to read. Across the hall was a drawing room where he could sit and read or paint, and upstairs were three large bedrooms. But the strangest thing was that each room had three bunk beds inside, but they were all empty, reminding Ernie that he was well and truly alone.

Outside the house was a large, luscious plant for him to spend all day feasting on. And as if that wasn't enough, there was also a big round bowl which was always full to overflowing with all kinds of wonderful vegetable and fruit scraps. It really was idyllic. However, as nice as all this 'stuff'

was, Ernie just wasn't at ease. Something about it just seemed too perfect, too unnatural and too far away from his dreams.

For a start, he was in a human kitchen in a human house, and that is just not right for a snail. What was even more disturbing was the fact that he still hadn't figured out who the two people were or what they wanted from him. There was only one thing he was certain of: he didn't trust them.

Then there was the fridge, which he had named the 'Big White Box'. It stood looming above him, right next to his window sill. He looked up at it and felt a shiver run across his shell as it towered over him, casting a dark shadow over his new little snail world. It was the fridge that he had found himself in last week, and he had no plans to find himself inside it ever again. He tried desperately to forget the ordeal, but every time they opened it a strong blast of icy cold wind would rush towards him, and if he was not stuck down it would blow him high into the air. Over the last week he had cleverly learnt to survive this windstorm by using his best suction power to cling to his plant whenever he saw someone approaching the fridge. He watched them visit that awful white box several times every day and wondered what they kept in it. However, he had decided that it was a waste of energy to think about that. All he cared about was finding a way to escape this situation before he found himself in a worse one.

He considered his new surroundings once more and realised how out of his depth he felt. Ernie was a dreamer. And a determined dreamer at that. Once he had set his heart on something he would do everything in his power to make it happen, no matter where it led him. But right now it seemed that following his dreams had led him all the way to a dead end. He knew that he had to escape, yet after a whole week he was still puzzled and no closer to devising a cunning plan.

Ernie sees daylight

Ernie's tentacles hung down to the floor. His situation seemed hopeless, and the thought of escaping was slipping away. It wasn't long before he heard the sound of footsteps coming into the kitchen again. His heart was so full of gloom that he didn't even bother to hide; he just continued to stare out of the window, feeling sorry for himself. Suddenly the fridge door was opened. Ernie didn't have time to stick to the window sill. He was swept into the air and came plummeting down, landing on the end of a leaf on his plant.

As he hung on his leaf, Ernie's head drooped in despair. 'What do these people want with me?' he mumbled as he stared at the floor far below him. Just then he heard a buzzing from behind him, becoming louder and louder. 'Gotta get outa here!' came a panicky voice. Ernie turned just in time to see a fly buzzing straight towards him. 'Incoming fly! Make way!!' He ducked but it was too late. The fly landed, slap bang, in his face. After an awkward pause, it flew off  towards the window, leaving Ernie stunned and dangling precariously on the very tip of the leaf, hanging by just one tentacle.

'What you doing, blocking my flight path?' the fly grumbled as he rearranged his crumpled wings. Ernie watched in amazement as the fly prepared to launch himself through the window. 'What are you doing?' shouted Ernie, clinging on to the leaf for dear life. 'Gotta get outa here,' buzzed the fly again.

Thud. 'Ouch!' Thud. 'Ouch!' Thud. 'Ouch!' Ernie watched as he flew into the glass again and again in an attempt to escape. 'That's got to hurt,' Ernie mumbled to himself. 'He must be crazy!'

'It is you who is crazy, my slimy amigo!' buzzed the fly.

'Don't you know that you can't escape?' Ernie replied, beginning to slip off the leaf. The fly stopped and looked back at him.

'Oh! It is you! You slimy slug, you the one stealing all the food.'

Ernie looked at him, puzzled. 'I am not a slug,' he said crossly, 'and I have no idea what you are talking about.'

 As Ernie struggled to regain his grip, the fly few over and buzzed around his tentacles. 'You nothing but pampered little pet!' Ernie forgot about his immediate danger of falling off the leaf and tried with all his might to swat the fly with his other tentacle.

'Ooh, you think you clever, but I am fast, and I am free. Two things you are not!' he buzzed as he flew to the window and continued to fly into the glass. 'But now you a pet you can be my new amigo … although you a little squishy. Anyway, enough of this nonsense, I am on important fly mission. I have people to see and places to be. Ooh that rhymes. I could be famous.' The fly started humming to himself as he continued to fly into the glass. 'Do you know the way to San José ... do … do … do dooo…!!' he sang.

Ernie suddenly spotted that the top window was open. 'Up there! The window is open,' he yelled, relieved to have a way to get rid of him.

The fly stopped and looked up. 'Oh yeah... thanks!' he said as he buzzed his way along the glass up to the open window, still humming his song. 'Adios, my slimy little pet slug!!' he said, laughing as he buzzed out of the window.

'I am not a slug!!' Ernie shouted as loudly as he could. Enviously he watched the fly enjoy his freedom as he dived and twisted with delight into the clear blue sky.

There was a moment's silence as he tried to make sense of it all, then suddenly he figured it out and yelled, 'I am a PET?!!' His boggly eyes nearly popped off his head. And with that he fell right off the leaf and landed, splosh, on the mud in his plant pot. At first he couldn't believe it, and he certainly didn't want to believe it. But the more he thought about it, the more it made sense. He sat in shock for a few moments, hoping he was wrong, but whichever way he looked at, it the fly seemed to be right. He looked around at his perfect home, and suddenly it all seemed so obvious. 'That's it!' he cried, 'That's why I am here. I have been kidnapped and made into a pet snail!'

Ernie was now in shock. He was rooted to the spot and covered in mud. His tentacles hung so low that they dragged in the sludge. The very idea was unimaginable. He thought back to his family and could almost hear his brothers laughing at him and saying, 'We told you so,' and 'We always knew you were a failure,' or his Mama saying, 'That's what you get for being a dreamer. Why couldn't you have been happy with a normal snail life like everyone else? You're always trying to prove stuff, Ernie; now look where it's got you.'

'ARGGGGHHHH! ENOUGH!' he shouted with all of his strength. He knew what it meant to be a pet. He had heard stories of how animals vanished and were never seen again. Soon he began to wish that he didn't know the truth. Wearily, he slumped against the plant pot and

25

sighed. Ernie liked being free, and he knew that snails were meant to be free. He sat in silence, feeling defeated and alone. 'This is not good at all,' he mumbled.

Then, from somewhere, he heard a voice: 'You can do this, Ernie. Don't give up.'

'Papa?!' he said, feeling confused and looking around him. But there was no one there. Then a wonderful feeling of peace began to stir in his heart and courage bubbled up inside him. For some reason that he didn't quite understand he no longer felt alone. It was as though he was being encouraged to believe in his dreams despite his situation. Instantly he felt better. With a new-found strength he got up and shouted, 'No! I will not become a pet. I refuse to, and I believe I stand for all snails everywhere. Snails do not make good pets! ...And neither do they make for good food in posh restaurants,' he added. Something had changed in Ernie's heart. It was as if knowing the truth about his situation had set him free, and now he was determined to escape. 'I will reach the Olive Garden, I know it. Nothing will get in my way.'

Just at that moment, one of his 'owners' walked into the kitchen carrying a huge jar of green Spanish olives – Ernie's favourite – and she dropped the largest olive he had ever seen into his bowl. Suddenly there was a tapping at the window. Ernie looked around and saw the fly buzzing outside the window and staring at the olive, his eyes large with delight. Ernie looked back at the olive and stared at it in amazement. His mouth began to water and his tentacles danced on his head. 'Let me in, amigo. I can't resist olives,' pleaded the fly. Ernie just ignored him. To him there was nothing tastier in the whole world than a scrumptious, juicy, mouth-wateringly good, green olive.

Tempting green olives

Many days had passed, and in between fighting off the fly who had found his way back in through the window, Ernie had been enjoying tucking into green olives day and night. He hadn't forgotten about escaping and was still determined to reach his dreams, but he had convinced himself that it was OK to finish at least half the jar first. After all, it wasn't every day that he was able to take advantage of a lifetime's supply of his favourite food. As the days went on he secretly began to enjoy this new life, and the thought of escaping became less urgent. Life as a pet was beginning to be more tempting than facing another journey into the unknown. However, with every olive he ate, he found it increasingly harder to fit inside his small shell. Ernie was getting fat!

As he stared at the reflection of his bulging belly in the window, he frowned. 'You slugs are crazy!' buzzed the fly as he flew irritatingly around Ernie's head. 'You keep eating olives you start to look like olive,' he said as he laughed in Ernie's ear. Ernie tried to swat him, but it was no good – he was too out of shape.

'Something has got to be done,' he mumbled to himself, watching his belly wobble as he prodded it with his tentacles.

'That's OK. Soon you go "pop" and there will be more olives for me,' buzzed the fly. Ernie began to feel dizzy as his eyes followed the fly while it spun in fast circles around his tentacles.

'THAT'S IT!' Ernie shouted. 'I am going on snail boot camp!' Desperately he looked around the kitchen for a training area big enough. Immediately his eyes landed upon the dreaded 'Big White Box'. He shuddered with fear. But as he could not think of a better option, he decided that it was time to overcome his fridge phobia and use it for his training ground. Either that or he would spend a lifetime being harassed by an annoying fly.

'Phew!' he said, as he puffed and panted his way through his ninth lap. 'Only one more to go.' He was barely able to get his words out.

'You nearly there, amigo. But you will never be fast as me. I am super fast. Look, I fly like lightning. Whooo! Now you see me, now you don't. Ooooh! Can you see me? NO!! I don't think so. I too fast for your boggly eyes.' Ernie rolled his eyes and tried to ignore him. 'You eat too much and you too wobbly to be speedy, Mr Gonzales. Up 2, 3, 4, keep it up, 2, 3, 4 … This boot camp is good idea. You call me Captain Pablo!'

Ernie used all the energy he had left to slide faster in an attempt to get away from him. By the time he finished his workout he was so exhausted that he didn't even notice his owners opening the fridge door. Caught off guard, the strong icy wind came howling over the top and swept him high into the air. He hovered for a few seconds and then came plummeting down, heading straight for the big gap between

the fridge and the wall.
'Arrrrgggggghhhhhhh!' he
screamed as he fell into the
darkness. Frantically, his
tentacles squirmed in all
directions trying to find
something to hold on to.
At last they hooked over a
wire and grabbed it tightly.

Swinging in the air he caught his breath. 'Crumbs!! That
was a close call.' As he looked down at the long drop below
him, something in the dark depths caught his eye. It seemed to
be the shell of a snail. Ernie's heart began to beat wildly with
excitement as he held tightly on to the wire. 'Hello!' he
shouted, but there was no answer. He pulled himself further
along until he could see more clearly, and to his amazement he
saw hundreds of snails. Ernie couldn't believe it – a whole
snail family. 'It's great to meet you. My name is Ernie,' he
called out again, but still there was no answer. Ernie was so
puzzled that he didn't even notice his tentacles beginning to
slip off the wire, and just as he was about to call out again, he
fell. 'Help!' he yelled as he hurtled down into the darkness and
crashed onto the shells.

There was a deadly silence. Something wasn't right. The hollow noise the shells made when he landed on them gave Ernie an eerie feeling in the pit of his stomach. He began to feel very uneasy. Bravely, Ernie looked inside one shell after another, and what he saw made his heart stop: they were all empty! Everywhere, more than he could count, empty snail shells were piled high and gathering dust behind the fridge. This meant only one thing: dead snails, and hundreds of them.

'NOOOO!!' yelled Ernie at the top of his lungs. The truth hit him like a large brick, and he realised he had been weak and easily tempted. 'How could I have allowed myself to enjoy being a pet?' He felt so stupid. 'I thought I was stronger than this!' He couldn't believe that he had put his dreams to one side just to eat olives. 'If I stay here I will just end up as nothing more than an empty snail shell behind a fridge in some human's house,' he said, feeling angry with himself. 'This is not "it". This is not my dream, and this is not what I am going to settle for.' As quickly as he could, he slid across the shells and stuck himself onto the side of the fridge.

The top was so far away he could barely see it. He had never travelled that far before, but somehow he managed to slide to the top, down the other side and onto the window sill in record time. It was as if he had gained supernatural strength. Once he reached his plant, he slid inside his house and began packing his stuff into his rucksack. It was time to start his new life of freedom, and he decided that whatever challenges lay ahead of him on his journey, he was prepared to face them bravely and boldly. Finally he was ready, and he felt more determined and stronger than ever.

First step to freedom

Ernie had to think quickly. As he scanned the kitchen, his
mind raced to think of an escape plan. Suddenly, his eyes
landed on a large green olive that was waiting for him to feast
upon, and a crazy idea came to mind. He didn't think; he just
got busy. Carefully he hollowed out the inside of the olive,
and then, when the hole was big enough, he squeezed himself
inside it.

Ernie waited patiently for
his owners to come and
change his food bowl. He had
watched them do it a hundred
times so he knew they would
soon sweep the leftover food
into the rubbish bin, and
eventually they would empty
its contents out of the window
onto the compost heap below.
With his head poking out of
the centre of the olive, he had
a perfect view of the entire
kitchen, and it wasn't long

before he saw one of them and heard the familiar sound of
footsteps coming towards him. Immediately he popped inside
his shell, inside the olive. Sure enough, just as he had
anticipated, his owner scooped him up along with his
leftovers and carried him across the kitchen. Ernie poked his
head out slightly and could see his owner's feet walking along
the red tiled floor towards the brown bin. His head bobbed up
and down with every step she took. 'Perfect!' he whispered,

excited at the thought of one of his plans finally working. Then, whoosh, she threw him into the bin.

As soon as everything was quiet and Ernie was sure that she had gone, he squeezed himself out of the olive. After he had dug his way out from under the pile of scraps, he sat on the heap of food and looked around. There was scrap after scrap of glorious snail delights. He took a deep breath and inhaled the sweet smell of rotting vegetables.

'Hola!' came a familiar voice from behind him. 'What you doing, my little slimy green amigo?' buzzed the fly.

Ernie let out a frustrated sigh. 'I am leaving this place, and I suggest you do the same. But don't follow me; I don't want you buzzing around me like a bad smell any more,' he said, hoping that soon he would finally be free of the fly and his pet home once and for all.

'Oh, I see. Now you slim you get feisty. You want fight with Captain Pablo?'

Ernie ignored him. He looked up to the top of the bin and, to his delight, the lid was open. His dream to get to snail paradise lay before him, and he was not going to let anyone or anything stop him from achieving his dreams.

'Oooooh, I see you going to escape. You will never reach the top. You just silly green slug. But I race you. See you there!'

Ernie quickly grabbed a snack of cabbage and avocado before beginning his ascent to the top of the bin. He knew he had to move fast, otherwise he would find himself squashed under another pile of scraps.

It was midday and it was hot. Ernie felt sweat running down his small head, but he kept going. He looked back at the trail he had made. Once again he was surprised at his speed, in spite of the heavy rucksack on his back that was pulling him down, and failed attempts to swat the fly that seemed intent on trying to distract him. He was determined that this time nothing was going to hold him back.

Finally he reached the top of the bin and took a deep breath. He felt rather proud of his efforts, but he knew that once he shook off the extra weight he had gained he would be able to go even faster. Now all he needed to do was to wait until someone came to empty the rubbish.

All this waiting was hard work, so Ernie decided to take a much-deserved rest on the rim of the bin. In no time at all he had fallen into a deep sleep, dreaming of the Olive Garden and living in an olive as big as a house.

Food, glorious food!

Ernie awoke with a jolt and found himself flying through the air. He watched in shock as trees and sky whooshed past him, and he hurtled towards the ground at great speed. As he looked back he caught a glimpse of his owners as they shook the last vegetable scrap out of the bin and closed the window. 'Ha!' he said smugly to himself, as he landed with a soft bump and bounced a few times. Ernie found himself sitting on a giant compost heap – a wonderland of vegetable scraps. There were trees everywhere and the beautiful river flowed before him. The sky was a clear blue with a tinge of orange sunrise as the day was dawning. It was such a beautiful sight.

Ernie breathed in the fresh, crisp air and realised that he must have been asleep since lunchtime the previous day. He must have needed it after his adventures, and he felt refreshed after such a good rest. With delight he sat on a soft banana skin and enjoyed watching the morning sun as it made its way over the leafy trees. He was happy, even though he had no idea where he was going, what adventures lay ahead of him or how he would find his way to his paradise land, but at least he knew that he had followed his heart and had made his escape. 'Nothing scares me any more – I am ready for anything,' he thought, as he lay back in the sun.

'You are trespassing on private property and you have ten seconds to leave, or I will charge!' The voice came out of nowhere in the silence of the early morning. Ernie jumped. It was a loud and frightening voice, and it caused the tiny hairs on his head to stand on end. Just as he was about to run in terror the voice bellowed again: 'Um, when I say "charge", I don't mean I will make you pay... Um, well, I will make you pay. What I mean is, I will CHARGE – run forward, that is, AND I WILL SQUASH YOU WITH MY BARE HANDS!'

Ernie looked puzzled. Something about the voice didn't seem right. Bracing himself to run as fast as his little snail body would carry him, he bravely turned around, expecting to see a giant, scary creature. But to his surprise, he came face to face with the open end of a large milk carton. Peering at him from inside it were two boggly eyes, not very different from his own. 'CHARGE!!!' boomed the voice again. Ernie's tentacles were blown back from the force, but he didn't budge. Instead, he folded his tentacles and stood his ground.

Eventually, a pair of green, slimy tentacles peered out of the milk carton, followed by the rest of a snail. 'G'day!' said the other snail sheepishly. 'I'm Bruce.'

Ernie smiled and replied, 'I'm Ernie. Nice to meet you.'
Bruce slid across carrot peelings and cabbage leaves to where
Ernie was, and they greeted each other by shaking tentacles.
Bruce looked slightly embarrassed at his failed attempt to
scare the intruder off his property. Ernie's heart was still
pounding a little from shock, but he was so glad to finally
meet another snail after being alone all this time.

Bruce was a large, slightly unusual-looking snail. He had
covered his shell in bits of green food that he had found on the
compost heap, and on his head he wore what looked like an
army hat, which was actually just half of a cherry pip. Ernie
thought that if he didn't look too closely, Bruce could look like
an army snail, if there was such a thing. He wasn't sure if there
was. An army ant, yes – but an army snail? 'No, snails are far
too peaceful to have armies,' he thought, but he couldn't help
chuckling to himself at Bruce's dress sense and his funny
attempts to scare him off the compost heap.

A sparkle of adventure

By now the sun was getting lower in the sky, and the hours passed quickly as the two snails chatted. Bruce told Ernie about how he had arrived from Australia. He had wedged himself in the grooves on the sole of a large boot to escape from a deadly hairy spider. But when he tried to wriggle free from the boot he discovered that he was stuck. Before he knew it he was on a flight from Australia to Spain. He managed to survive for two whole weeks by eating bits of vegetation off the floor, until eventually, to his relief, the owner threw the boots over the wall onto this compost heap. Bruce told Ernie of his amazement when he finally managed to pop himself out and discovered that he was on a huge pile of food.

'Wow! What an awful ordeal,' said Ernie, thinking that Bruce's traumatic story made his problems seem small.

'Yeah, but look where I ended up. This place is a never-ending heap of vegetable scraps. What snail could ask for more?' Bruce said as his eyes grew larger with the sheer wonder of his home. To Bruce, this place was heaven; he would never have to go looking for food again, and he would defend it at any cost. Ernie looked around. It really was amazing – an Aladdin's treasure trove of snail goodies.

Ernie then began to tell Bruce his own story: of the day he left home, his eventful journey in a vegetable box and how he was almost squashed between two beetroots. Bruce shuddered at the thought. Ernie then told him about his visit to the vegetable market and how he had found himself in the fridge of someone's house. When he shared with Bruce about the empty snail shells behind the fridge, and how he realised that he had been taken captive as a pet snail, his new friend looked terrified and was speechless. Ernie continued the story of his escape, right up to their meeting, and described the joy he was feeling as they sat together on the glorious vegetable mound, knowing that he was finally free.

Bruce listened with interest as his tentacles jiggled around on his head. He was an adventurous snail and was captivated by the story and intrigued by Ernie's determination. However, he couldn't help wondering why he had set out on such a crazy journey in the first place. Ernie could almost see the question running through Bruce's mind but was reluctant to tell him about the Olive Garden. For a moment he hesitated; he couldn't bear it if Bruce were to laugh at him for believing in his dreams. But then he remembered his new-found strength and decided that it really didn't matter what other people thought. After all, *he* believed, and that was all that really mattered. He took a deep breath and then, with passion and excitement, he told Bruce all about his Papa, how their ancestors came from a paradise garden long ago and how he and his Papa dreamed of finding it again. He took great delight in describing it in every detail, just as his Papa had described it to him when he was a small snail.

'So that's where I am going. And no matter what challenges I face, I *will* get there,' finished Ernie. Bruce's eyes were nearly popping out of his head, and his wide, slimy jaw dropped in wonder and awe. He was fascinated by Ernie's faith in his dreams, despite so many obstacles, although deep down he didn't really believe that there was such an Olive Garden. With so much to think about, the two snails sat in silence, looking up at the stars and munching on a cabbage leaf.

'Do you *really* think it exists?' asked Bruce, after a long silence.

'Of course I do. I know it does,' replied Ernie. 'It has to,' he thought, 'otherwise all of this has been for nothing.' Suddenly an idea came to him and he turned to Bruce, who had his mouth full of cabbage. 'You should come with me, Bruce, and we can find it together!'

Bruce nearly choked on the cabbage. 'Me?! You want *me* to go with you? Thanks for the offer, mate, but I belong here. This place is fair dinkum. It's good enough for me.' With that he folded his tentacles. 'You're on your own. But I wish ya the best of luck,' he added, trying to look as though he meant it. But Ernie could see a little sparkle of adventure glowing in his eyes.

The two new friends decided to call it a night. Bruce went back to his milk carton and Ernie snuggled down on the soft banana skin. He fell asleep under the stars with a warm feeling in his heart. It had been a long and tiring day, but he was free now, and although he had no idea how or when he would reach his dreams, something in his heart told him that he would, and that was enough for him. He fell into a peaceful sleep with a smile on his face.

Ready with nowhere to go

The next morning, Ernie awoke as daylight crept across his face. He stretched his long neck and wiggled his tentacles. It was going to be a good day – he could feel it. As he rolled over to get up, there standing over him was Bruce with his cherry pip army hat still sitting proudly on his small head. 'G'day, cobber! If we're gonna find this Olive Garden of yours then we'd better get moving, or half the day will be gone.' Ernie couldn't believe what he was hearing.

Despite Bruce's disbelief in Ernie's story, overnight he had given it some thought and decided that the least he could do was help his fellow snail on his way, even if it was the way to nowhere! Then at least he could have his compost heap all to himself again.

Ernie jumped up with delight. 'That's the spirit!' he said, looking at Bruce excitedly. 'But I'm not going anywhere until you find me a hat like yours... Oh, and not until we've had breakfast. True adventurers don't go anywhere on empty stomachs,' said Ernie, feeling delighted.

'Yeah! Sure thing, mate,' replied Bruce, in his strong Australian accent.

Quickly they munched on a few figs and avocados and then Bruce rummaged through the food scraps to find his friend an army hat. Ernie proudly put on his new hat, swung his rucksack onto his shell and they were ready to go.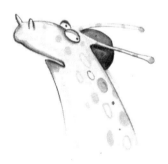

'So where are we going?' asked Bruce.

'That's a very good question,' answered Ernie, looking slightly puzzled. 'We need to head downstream, and it should be there… somewhere.' Ernie didn't really have a clue how he was going to find the Olive Garden, let alone how they would get down the river, but he didn't want Bruce to know that. The river, which stretched out before them, appeared to branch off in two directions. Ernie's plan had originally seemed so simple: over the wall with the leftover vegetables, a leisurely slide down to the river bank and then a gentle sail down the river to his garden. But now that plan seemed silly as he looked at the river and tried to decide which way would lead them safely there.

All of a sudden they heard a rustling from the trees behind them, followed by a sniffing. 'FREEZE! Don't move!' Bruce said, sounding panicked.

Ernie held his breath. 'What is it?'

'Shhh!!' replied Bruce. 'We need to be quiet.'

The sniffing stopped. Then there were footsteps, except they weren't human footsteps. Ernie's heart began to beat fast as he realised that they were the padding steps of wild dogs, and as every snail knows only too well, wild dogs are always hungry and will eat anything they can get their paws on, including snails.

'OK, I have a plan,' whispered Bruce who had escaped from wild dogs many times before. 'See that large cabbage leaf over there?' Ernie looked to where Bruce's tentacle was pointing. 'When I tell you, we move towards it and slide under it. Then slowly we make our way to the river with it on our heads, turn it over, jump on it and sail downstream.'

Ernie was impressed. 'Good plan,' he said. 'Let's go!'

They slid quickly across the scraps and slipped easily under the leaf. 'Phew!' said Ernie. Immediately they began moving towards the river, making a zigzag trail as they went. It took them a while to work out how to head in the same direction and for a while they went around in circles. They were in such a panic they didn't notice the dogs drawing nearer.

One of them came and stood hovering over the snails, cocking his head from one side to the other, looking puzzled as he watched the cabbage leaf moving on its own. His pack had now caught up, and they rummaged around behind him, eating scraps.

'Almost there!' whispered Bruce, as they touched the cool water of the river's edge. When they had caught their breath, Bruce shouted, 'Now!' They flung the leaf off their heads into the river. Then as fast as they could, they jumped onto it. Ernie was impressed at Bruce's speed and agility, and wondered if he did circuit training too. The wild dog stood watching, even more puzzled. 'Paddle as fast as you can!' shouted Bruce. He had seen the giant dog staring at them, and feared he might pounce on them at any moment. Using their tentacles, both snails paddled as hard as they could in a desperate attempt to escape.

'Hola amigos!' came a buzzing voice.

'Oh no! You're the fly from the house. Buzz off. I'm busy!' panted Ernie.

'Ooh, you two amigos are cool. I saw you sliding away from dogs. It was quick escape. Nice moves.'

Ernie couldn't believe it; he thought he had seen the last of the fly when he escaped from the house. 'There's no way you are coming with me,' he said in frustration.

'You can't stop me, speedy, I want come with you. I be Captain Pablo and I lead boat. Follow me!' he buzzed.

'What are you doing, Ern?! Why aren't you paddling?!' shouted Bruce from the front of the leaf, fast getting out of breath.

'I just have to do something first,' replied Ernie, trying to swat the fly away. Finally his tentacles hit their target, and he sent him spinning off towards the dogs.

'Nooo! I too young to be dog's breakfast… Arrgh!!'

The dog, feeling lazy in the warm summer sun, watched curiously as the two snails floated down the river on the leaf. 'KEEP PADDLING!' shouted Bruce, his heart almost pounding out of his chest. Ernie was paddling as fast as his small tentacles could go. The snails didn't dare to look behind them in case the dog was hot on their trail, but by now he had rejoined his pack and was enjoying some breakfast and the thought of a long morning nap.

The rapids

Eventually Bruce stopped paddling. 'Far out, mate!' he said, as
he relaxed back on the leaf. 'That was a close one.' Ernie
looked around him. They were far away from the river bank,
and Bruce's beloved compost heap was almost out of sight.
The river was beautifully peaceful and calm, and there was a
gentle breeze pushing them forward. Now all they had to do
was to decide which way to go – to the left or to the right.
Ernie studied the options for a while. The left side of the river
flowed along a wall and the river seemed to be moving faster
than on the right side, which looked to be very calm and
pleasant, although he couldn't see quite where it led to. Ernie
had no idea which way to go and they had to decide soon. He
looked at Bruce, who also looked unsure. 'Right!' said Bruce. 'I
think we should go right – it looks calmer and safer.'

Ernie agreed. He had had enough action for one morning
and thought it best to play safe. 'Good choice, my friend. Let's
go for it!' Ernie said, and the cabbage leaf continued to drift
down the river in the bright Spanish sunshine.

'This is the life!' Ernie said as he closed his eyes and
imagined drifting in his very own boat across Lemon Harbour.
Bruce began to relax as well. He thought that it was good to
have company after such a long time, and he decided to make
the most of this little excursion.

Suddenly the leaf hit something hard underneath it and the
'boat' stopped moving. Dazed, the snails looked around to
figure out what had happened. Water began to spill over into
the cabbage leaf. 'We're stuck and taking on water!' shouted
Bruce.

'I know! But I can't see what's stopped us,' Ernie yelled in
panic as he turned to look at Bruce, hoping he would have an

answer. But Bruce had vanished! Ernie was baffled. 'Bruce, where are you?'

He could hear gurgling coming from the water behind him and he looked over the edge of the leaf. There was his friend splashing around and about to sink to the river bed. For a second, Ernie froze, feeling powerless to help. 'Look in your rucksack!' gurgled Bruce as he vanished beneath the surface. Ernie sprang into action. Flinging open his trusted old rucksack he emptied its contents into the boat. 'Umm, cotton bud, blob of sticky chewing gum, mint, yo-yo, sketch pad, pencil.' Ernie sighed. 'What was I thinking?' he mumbled, wishing he had given it more thought before packing such useless items.

Suddenly a crazy idea came to him. Grabbing the chewing gum, he quickly stuck one side of it to the mint and the other to the floor of the leaf. Then he flung the mint out into the water. 'Grab on, Bruce!' he yelled, the pink chewing gum stretching behind the mint as it flew through the air. All of a sudden, Bruce, who was under the water and sinking fast, saw a round object with a hole in the middle coming towards him.

He reached out, grabbed it and put his head through the middle as Ernie hauled him up. Bruce landed, coughing and spluttering, back on the leaf. 'Wow! That was close, too close, Bruce. Don't ever do that to me again!' Ernie panted.

Bruce smiled and patted his friend on his shell. 'Good on ya mate! You did good, Ern. That was quick thinking, real Aussie style – I like it! I think I'll call you the fastest snail in the west from now on.' Ernie laughed at his friend's sense of humour. 'Let's get this boat moving and get on with some hard yakka,' Bruce added, shaking himself dry. Ernie had no idea what 'hard yakka' meant but was just glad his friend was safe.

Bruce tapped his tentacles on the bottom of the boat and felt something hard underneath it. 'We must be stuck on a large rock. Start paddling and we'll soon be moving again.' But just then the two snails felt the cabbage leaf wobble. 'We seem to be on the move already!' shouted Bruce. Slowly the cabbage leaf lifted up out of the water and began moving forward in the air.

Ernie peered over the edge. 'Hey! We're not just on any rock – we're on a moving rock!'

Bruce looked pale. 'Ern, that's not possible. Rocks don't just move on their own.'

'Well this one *DOES*!!' yelled Ernie.

'ARRRRRGGGGHHHHH!!' they both shouted. Ernie clung to the side of the leaf with one tentacle and to his friend with the other.

'What's going on?!' shouted Bruce.

'I have no idea, but hold on tight,' Ernie replied as he pointed towards the fast, rushing river that lay before them. Bruce had only seconds to grab hold of Ernie before they entered the rapids. Violently they were flung from side to side with the force of the water as they held on using the strongest suction power they could muster.

The two hitchhikers

The rapids were strong and powerful. Walls of water towered above them before crashing down over them. A huge wave almost flipped the leaf over completely, but somehow they managed to come through it safely. The water gushed around and over large rocks, and with each new wave the snails closed their eyes, expecting the worst, but the worst never came. It was as if someone was carrying them, holding them up and keeping them safe.

Eventually the rapids died away and they floated out into calm water. The snails were still clinging to the leaf in terror, and the stuff from Ernie's rucksack was strewn across the now soggy cabbage leaf. Ernie looked over at his friend who was munching on the side of the boat.

'What are you doing?' asked Ernie.

'I always eat when I'm nervous,' Bruce replied.

'Look at that!' Ernie had spotted something moving under their boat. At first he thought it was a fish, but it seemed to be making the same movement again and again – disappearing then returning.

'Hey look, Ern, there's one over this side too,' said Bruce. Ernie looked; it was just the same. The snails stared at each other with a puzzled look, and then smiled. Together they slid to the front of the soggy cabbage leaf and peered over the edge. Sure enough, there it was, just as they expected: a head with two beady eyes on a long, thick neck, attached to a magnificent and graceful turtle. They chuckled. They had figured out the mystery of the moving rock.

'Good morning,' they said.

The turtle looked up in surprise. 'Hey! What are you doing on my back?'

'Er, I'm terribly sorry,' replied Ernie. 'This is rather embarrassing, but I have no idea.'

Bruce butted in. 'Yeah, but cheers for the lift, mate. We wouldn't have got through those rapids back there without ya.'

The turtle smiled at the two small snails sitting on his back with cherry pip hats on their heads. 'De nada!' he said cheerfully. 'Encantado. Me llamo José.'

'Nice to meet you, José. I'm Ernie, and this is my good friend and fellow adventurer, Bruce. So where are you travelling to today?' asked Ernie confidently.

'I am on my way to see my family downstream; they live just under the fig trees. And where are you amigos going?' José asked as he glided effortlessly down the river. 'Is there anywhere I can drop you off?'

'Well, that is a very good question. We are looking for a special place called Olive Garden. Do you know it?' enquired Ernie tentatively.

José turned to his new friends and grinned. 'Yes, I do. Very well, in fact. My family lives near there. It is a beautiful place.' Ernie couldn't believe it. He was so happy that his tentacles began dancing excitedly on his small head. He turned to smile at Bruce, but Bruce had fainted; it was all too much for him.

Paradise found

Bruce was woken by the strong, sweet smell of lemons. He squinted as he opened his eyes. The sun was shining brightly and there was not a cloud in the sky. He leapt up and looked around – the sight was magnificent. Before him lay endless olive trees and a pool of tranquil, clear, blue water. 'I must be dreaming,' he mumbled, but just as he was about to lay down and go to sleep again he heard a splashing coming from the pool. He looked up and, to his surprise, there was Ernie, heading towards him on a leaf boat.

'Jump on board, my friend. It looks like I was right about this olive place.' Bruce was speechless as he slid on board alongside his friend. 'And it's even better than I imagined. Are you ready to check out Lemon Harbour? They have a special of

"Cabbage à la Sprouts" on the menu tonight.'

'Ernie, this place is awesome. Is it for real? This is the best billabong I've ever set my eyes on,' Bruce said as he looked around at the stunning lake. He sat staring in amazement as Ernie sailed the boat across the crystal clear water.

Bruce and Ernie spent day after day in paradise, soaking up the sun, enjoying the pool and feasting on endless olives. Time flew by as the friends explored and enjoyed their new home. Bruce soon forgot all about his old compost heap of rotting vegetable scraps and settled in to his new home like a king in a palace. They became good friends with José, who was very wise and visited them often. Life was good for the two brave adventurers. They seemed to have everything they needed, and more.

However, Ernie gradually began to notice a restless feeling growing in his heart. He tried ignoring it and eating more olives, but it just wouldn't go away. His friend seemed to be

 content and was good enough company, but he was growing more and more unsettled. It was as if he felt there was something else that he should be doing. He hated to admit it, but it felt like this Olive Garden was just not enough for him.

After a month of being in his new home, the feeling had grown so strong that Ernie couldn't concentrate on anything else, so he decided to go and visit José. He slid out of the garden and followed the river bank to José's house. They sat down to talk over a cup of nettle tea, and Ernie told him how he was feeling.

José listened with compassion and understanding. When Ernie had finished, Jose said, 'It seems quite clear to me that you have this feeling because you were meant for something bigger than the Olive Garden.'

Ernie looked at him, surprised. 'What do you mean?'

Jose continued, 'We weren't designed to live for only ourselves. This garden of yours is everything you have dreamed of, but it is not what you were made for. Ask yourself, is there something that you ran away from or turned your back on so that you could reach this dream garden?'

Ernie sat in silence. José's question made him feel slightly uncomfortable. He thanked his friend for his help and set off on the long slide back to the Olive Garden, mulling it all over as he went.

That night he dreamt about the empty snail shells behind the fridge. He woke up in a panic and sat bolt upright. A shiver ran through his small body. It was awful to think about the fate of those snails, and he wondered how many others were kept as pets, never to be seen again. 'That's it!' he yelled. 'How can I be happy here in paradise knowing there are hundreds of other snails out there being taken captive?'

Bruce, who was sleeping on a leaf in the middle of the pool, was awoken with a start when Ernie shouted. He jumped with shock and fell, splash, right into the water.

'Something has to be done, Bruce. We have to leave this very morning!' Ernie said with great determination.

'What?!' replied a soggy Bruce as he slid out of the water. 'I know I said I liked this billabong, but that didn't mean I wanted to swim in it.'

'Pack your bags, my friend. We have work to do. We're leaving,' stated Ernie. Bruce frowned as he shook the drips off his tentacles. He didn't like the sound of this.

Ernie explained everything as he packed his bag. Bruce listened in disbelief. 'You're on ya own with this one, mate. There's no way I'm leaving this place, not for anything or anyone.'

Ernie felt a little disappointed but he knew he had to go, with or without Bruce, though it would be a whole lot better with him. 'But Bruce, you're so brave, and you know the compost heap better than anyone else. And who will protect me from the dogs?' But Bruce would not be persuaded. So, hoisting on his rucksack, Ernie headed off to get some breakfast as the first light of the day broke through the trees.

A change of plan

Ernie sat at the Lemon Harbour café enjoying his last meal in the Olive Garden. 'It's so beautiful here,' he thought, as the most stunning sunrise filled the morning sky and was reflected in the pool. It was the first time he had felt at peace in a long time. He had now discovered a mission more worthwhile than fulfilling his own dreams, and he felt excited. He had to prevent any more snails being taken captive and ending up as empty shells behind a fridge in someone's kitchen, and if that meant saying goodbye to this place then it was a small sacrifice, and one that he was glad to make.

Bruce eventually joined him at the café. Mopily, he slid onto a chair at the table. 'OK, I'll help you, but ...' – Ernie didn't really like 'buts' – '... I'll only go with you as far as the compost heap. I'll set you off on your way and then I'm heading back here. If you decide to come back and join me some day, then you know where to find me.'

When he had finished speaking, Bruce sat back and folded his tentacles as if to say, 'End of discussion.' Ernie decided that was good enough for him. He knew that Bruce was a true adventurer at heart and now knew him well enough to expect that once he was involved he wouldn't turn back. As he ate his last mouthful of fig and apricot salad he took one last look around at the precious garden.

When there was enough light, the snails set off. First they had to head to José's house. They arrived just as the family of turtles were tucking into their own hearty breakfast. Ernie told José the whole story while José's wife prepared them a fresh Spanish omelette each. Ernie decided not to refuse a second breakfast and savoured the piping hot food.

José was pleased to help them out. 'Well done, Ernie, for figuring it out. I knew you had it in you to do something great. I am with you all the way. Just tell me what you would like me to do.'

Ernie smiled. He was so glad to have met José – he was such a good turtle. 'Just get us back to that compost heap please, my friend!'

'Sure thing, amigo,' said José. As soon as they had finished the delicious omelettes, the snails slipped up onto José's back and headed out into the river, upstream towards the compost heap.

'Stick on, my amigos!' shouted José, 'This is going to be a rough ride.' The snails didn't need to be told twice. Immediately they pulled out their best suction power and held on to each other with their tentacles. Moving against the stream was a whole different experience, but despite the current pulling them back they made it safely through.

'What now?' asked José. Ernie looked puzzled. He hadn't really thought any further than reaching Bruce's old home. The three friends stopped for a minute at the river's edge to catch their breath. They watched as a slow, and very smelly, rubbish truck made its way past the park along the bridge.

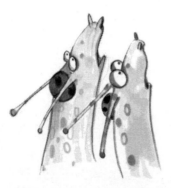

Suddenly Ernie shouted, 'That's where we're going! That's our ride!'

Bruce shot him a disapproving look. 'You've got to be kidding me!' he shouted. 'For one, there's no way we could make it up the wall of the bridge to the road. And even if we did, we'd be swallowed alive – have ya seen the mouth on that thing?' They stared into the open back of the rubbish truck, shuddering as its big metal jaws came crushing down effortlessly to devour everything inside it. 'Besides, you don't even have a plan. How do you think you're going to find hundreds of other snails, let alone bring them back to the Olive Garden, from the back of a rubbish truck?'

For a moment Ernie wondered if Bruce was right, but quickly he pulled himself together. 'I don't have a plan; I just have faith, and right now I believe that truck is our ride. Where to, I'm not sure, but it beats waiting here all day,' he said determinedly. 'I just have no idea how we're going to get up to it.'

Bruce looked at him in surprise. 'WE?!' he shouted. 'I don't remember there being a "we", only a "you".' And he began to slide back to the river.

'Bruce, wait! At least help me get up there, and then you can go back to the Olive Garden.'

Bruce stopped. His friend's new-found courage and determination was rather inspiring, even if it was also slightly crazy. 'You've gone bananas, mate! OK, OK. Just let me think for a minute,' and he sat down between Ernie and José.

Ernie was just about to get his trusted sketch pad out from his rucksack to brainstorm some ideas when he heard a familiar barking. Instantly they all froze. They looked up at the bridge and saw a pack of hungry looking dogs following the truck, hoping to catch some scraps for breakfast. One of the dogs caught the smell of the compost heap and began making

its way down a ramp towards them. It was the largest of the pack, with long legs and big teeth.

'Don't move!' said Bruce, as they all retreated into their shells. They watched as the dog ran back and forth between the road and the compost heap, hunting for the best scraps.

'I think your next ride is here, amigos!' came a muffled voice from inside José's thick shell. Both snails popped their heads out of their shells and looked at José, hoping they had heard wrong. 'It's easy. You are snails. You can stick to anything,' said José as he looked over at the dog.

'Now we know turtles are crazy!' said Ernie.

'Hang on a minute,' whispered Bruce. 'Maybe he's on to something. It's risky, but it could work.'

'WHAT?!' shouted Ernie, looking at Bruce and feeling decidedly irritated.

'All you need to do is attach yourself to the dog's paw and slide up his leg. Then just hold on until he goes back up onto the bridge, jump off and slip onto the truck. I'll be here to egg you on,' Bruce said. He made it sound so easy. 'What do you think?' he added, wearing his most convincing smile.

Ernie was not impressed. 'I think it's you who's gone bananas or whatever it was.' He was just about to get out his sketch pad so he could calculate the risk involved and the chances of it actually working, when the dog began to sniff a pile of leftovers right next to him.

'Now's your chance,' whispered José. 'I am off, guys. I will see you back in the Olive Garden. Hasta luego!' And with that he quietly slipped back into the river.

No time to waste

The two snails sat huddled in their mobile homes, staring at the seemingly impossible challenge that lay before them. Eventually Bruce popped his head out. 'Are you ready?'

Ernie looked at him blankly. 'OK, good. Let's jump!' and before Ernie could find the words to stop him, Bruce had attached himself to the dog's paw. 'Come on, Ern, quick! The dog will be heading back to the truck any second.'

Ernie knew he had no choice. He closed his eyes and thought about the empty shells behind the fridge. Then, with all the strength he could find, he stretched out his tentacles and jumped. He landed just on the edge of the dog's paw.

'Good on ya! Now pull yourself up or he'll squash ya!' shouted Bruce from the dog's other leg. Bravely, Ernie swung his small body around by his tentacles and hoisted himself safely on top of the paw, then quickly moved himself up the dog's leg. Both snails were now firmly attached to his back legs, just as he took off at full speed to chase the rubbish truck again.

The snails clung on tightly as the dog bounded away at full speed. 'Haaaannnggg oooooonnnnnn!!!' shouted Bruce, as they both used all the suction they could muster to stick to the dog's shiny fur.

'I thooooughtt yoouu weeerrren't comiiing,' said Ernie.

'I knnnow, mmeeee toooo!' replied Bruce.

'Meeee thhhrrrreeeee,' buzzed a little voice near Ernie's ear as the fly sped past him to catch up with the rubbish truck.

'Oh no! Not you again!' shouted Ernie.

The dog dashed around the corner and leapt over a fence. Little did he realise that he had two brave hitchhiking snails attached to his legs. Finally he skidded to a sharp stop as he joined the rest of the pack. They greeted each other playfully and then trotted off behind the truck as it pulled away up the hill. Ernie peered over at Bruce, who looked as if he had done this before. He thought that he probably had!

When the truck stopped to collect another bag of rubbish, the dogs began to eat the peelings which had fallen around the wheels. 'This is our stop, Ern. It's time to get off,' said Bruce.

Ernie had turned slightly pale and was feeling a little seasick from all the bounding, and didn't need telling twice. 'I'm right behind you my friend,' he shouted. He watched as Bruce slid down the dog's leg and up onto the tyre of the truck. Ernie was just about to follow him when the truck began to move.

'Bruce, watch out!' he shouted loudly. It appeared that his friend was about to be crushed under the wheel. Bruce had a split second to think of something before he came face to face with the hard concrete road, squashed between it and the huge truck tyre.

Ernie held his breath. The truck stopped and the bin men threw more bags into its mouth. 'Bruce, where are you?'

Ernie panicked. He couldn't see his friend anywhere. It didn't look good. Without hesitating he slid down the dog's leg and up onto the tyre. Then he worked his way up towards the wheel arch. He was almost there when he felt the wheel beginning to move as the truck drove off once more. The tyre turned, with Ernie on it. With speed he passed the wheel arch. He stretched up to grab hold of it but missed, and before he knew it he found himself heading rapidly towards the sun-scorched concrete road. 'Nnnooooo!' he cried. His adventure was about to come to a squishy end.

An unusual ride

It was a hot morning in the beautiful little village of Vinuella. All was quiet and peaceful except for the low rumbling of the rubbish truck as it wound its way up the steep hill through the old streets. People were beginning to set off for work and shops were starting to open. Everything was calm and peaceful, but for Ernie this was turning out to be his worst nightmare. His best friend had just been squashed, and it looked as if he was heading for the same disastrous fate. With all the strength he could find, he tried to slide himself up the tyre and away from the ground.

As the wheel continued to turn, Ernie could see that he was fast approaching the ground. He had to think of something quickly. Looking at the tyre he noticed deep grooves running all around the black rubber and remembered Bruce's story of how he had hidden in the tread of a big boot. Desperately, he wedged himself in the nearest groove and ducked inside his shell. Then he held his breath and waited.

Everything went dark and he wondered if he was going to survive as he felt the weight of the truck pushing him down against the hard concrete. But the groove was deep enough and within no time at all he glimpsed light through his shell. He popped his head out and looked up at the truck above him as the tyre continued to turn. To his amazement, there, sitting on the wheel arch, was Bruce. Ernie sighed with relief.

'Stretch out your tentacles. I'll pull you up,' Bruce called cheerily. Ernie reached out as far as he could but it was no good – he was stuck. Suddenly he felt the cotton bud in his

 rucksack prodding into his back and he had an idea. Reaching back, he

grabbed it and threw it up to Bruce.

'Try this!' he shouted. 'It might just work.' Bruce caught the cotton bud with both tentacles, and as his friend passed him in the tyre he slid it under Ernie's shell and pushed down on the other end as hard as he could. POP! Ernie burst out of the groove and flipped high into the air, before tumbling back down and landing, splat, right next to his buddy on the wheel arch.

'You ripper! That was a corker of a landing, Ern!'

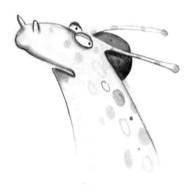

Ernie looked at Bruce, puzzled. 'What did you say?' he asked, baffled.

'Nice one, mate. I'm glad you could join me.' The pair looked at each other and burst out laughing. They laughed so much their bellies ached. Ernie had never laughed so much in his short life. When they finally stopped, he looked at his friend with pride.

'I really thought I'd lost you,' he said, realising that he couldn't do this without him.

'You can't get rid of me that easily. We have work to do!' Bruce said.

'I knew you'd come along,' said Ernie, as he slid his cherry pip hat neatly back on his head.

Bruce shot him an embarrassed look. 'What do you mean?' he said, slightly sheepishly.

'I know you can't say no to an adventure. I know you too well, Bruce.' And the two friends sat back on the wheel arch of the truck, giggling again as they watched the dogs running behind.

'Aren't you glad you're not a dog?' said Ernie.

'Sure am,' said Bruce. 'Having four feet must really get in the way,' he laughed. 'Yes, and I'm also glad I'm not a fly.

Look at that thing – the dog's going to gobble him up any minute.' They laughed as they watched the dog snap away at the fly who was buzzing teasingly around his ear.

It was midday when the rubbish truck finished its rounds and pulled into the depot at the top of the hill in Vinuella. The two snails had fallen asleep on the way. As they awoke the bin men were heading off for lunch, which would be followed by their usual afternoon siesta. The dogs were already dozing in the shade, enjoying a nap themselves.

Once everything was quiet, the snails slid down the side of the truck onto the hot road. 'Ouch, it's hot!' they yelled, as they danced up and down. 'Oh! Ouch! Ooooh! We've got to find some shade and some cool ground,' said Ernie. Bruce spotted a large rubbish bin at the edge of the road. He quickly rolled himself up into a ball and dived underneath it, closely followed by Ernie.

'Phew! It's much cooler under here. A few more seconds on that road and we would have been fried dog food.' Ernie shuddered at the thought and wished Bruce didn't have to be so descriptive. At least we're safe now, he thought, as he sat back in his shell and began to devise the next part of the plan: how to round up the snail population of Vinuella.

Time to play

Ernie pulled out his sketch pad and began jotting down some ideas as Bruce just sat, dazed but excited, his mind racing from the morning's adventures. Even though he still thought Ernie was crazy for leaving the Olive Garden, he was really enjoying their adventure. He looked over at Ernie, frantically scribbling on a large drawing pad and mumbling to himself. It appeared that he had no idea where they were and that he still didn't have the faintest clue as to how they were going to round up the other snails. But one thing was for sure: Ernie might not know how they were going do it, but he knew they *would* do it. Bruce was a little concerned at Ernie's lack of a plan, but he decided not to mention it just yet; something told him to trust his friend's faith and determination for a little longer.

Ernie stopped for a moment and looked down the road. From where they were at the top of the hill he could just about make out his family's house. He wondered if everyone was alright. He longed to see his Papa and tell him about all the things he had done. 'Whoa!! It's getting real hot, Ern,' said Bruce out of the blue, bringing Ernie back from his thoughts.

'Yeah, it seems like a warm breeze; it must be blowing off the ocean.'

Bruce looked at him, puzzled. 'We're nowhere near the ocean, ya goof.' The snails stopped talking and looked at each other in growing alarm. In the silence, directly behind them, they could hear the sound of deep, heavy breathing. Neither dared to turn around and look.

Suddenly, Ernie felt a sharp whack across the back of his shell. It sent him flying forward and skimming across the hard concrete surface. He just about had time to retreat inside the safety of his shell before he hit the wheel of the rubbish bin.

Smack!! Next, Bruce took a hit and also found himself bouncing and then rolling along the hot ground. He came to a stop in a pothole in the middle of the road. Dazed, Ernie poked his head out of his shell.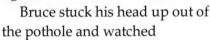
His cherry pip army hat had slid down and was covering his eyes. 'BRUCE! Where are you? It's gone dark!' he shouted at the top of his voice. 'Who turned off the lights?'

Bruce stuck his head up out of the pothole and watched helplessly as Ernie slid around in circles, unable to see where he was going. Bruce noticed something moving in the shadows under the bin. 'WATCH OUT!!' he yelled, as the creature prepared to pounce again. But it was too late. Ernie took another whack, only this time he flew up in the air and hit his head on the bottom of the bin. Thankfully his hard army hat protected his small head. He bounced a few times like a rubber ball, before taking another hit. Backwards and forwards he went. Ernie was soon so dizzy and confused he had no idea what was going on. He wondered if the world had ended, but before he could give it any more thought he was knocked out inside his shell.

Bravely, Bruce pulled himself out of the safety of the pothole. Cautiously, he made his way back to the bin. His friend was in danger and he had to do something, but he had no idea what he was dealing with. As he came nearer he saw four white paws and four ginger paws. 'Far out! It's CATS!' he whispered to himself. 'Ernie's in real danger.' As he crept closer he soon realised that it was even worse than he had first thought. Not only were they cats, but they were KITTENS, and very playful, boisterous kittens at that... and it was all too obvious that Ernie had become their new toy.

Bruce had to move fast and find a way to rescue him. He knew Ernie wouldn't be able to take much more of the kittens' 'play'. However, he had to be careful not to end up the same way. Just at that moment the ginger kitten spotted him. She crouched and prepared to pounce. 'What a day this is turning out to be,' muttered Bruce as he dived into his shell. With speed he rolled along the ground. Then all of a sudden the floor fell away from him and he felt himself falling. As he hit the floor he stuck his head out of his shell to see where he was. 'Great! I'm in another pothole,' he said, feeling completely useless. But as he spoke he noticed that his voice sounded strangely loud.

As he turned around he saw that he was right in front of an empty milk carton which had a large opening in the bottom, just like the one on his old compost heap. 'HELLO!' he boomed, as his voice echoed down the milk carton. 'Perfect!' he said. Then he climbed in, took a deep breath and cleared his throat. 'Listen up, ya mangey fleabags,' he thundered. 'That's my friend you're playing with, and I suggest you let him go and find another toy, or else!' He wasn't sure what 'else' would be, but hoped that they wouldn't think to ask.

The kittens immediately stopped what they were doing. Ernie came to in his shell and nervously poked his head out. 'Bruce, I'm OK. Where are you?' he said faintly.

'Over here, Ern,' Bruce whispered. Ernie couldn't see him anywhere, and wondered why his voice had sounded so loud. 'I'm in the carton, in the hole in the road. Come this way.' Hurriedly, Ernie pulled himself over to where the voice was coming from and slid into the pothole. By now the kittens were hiding behind their mum, who was enjoying her siesta. Hungrily, they tried to take milk from her, but there was very little left. None of them had eaten for days. They were frightened and desperate for food.

A crazy idea

Safely hidden in the pothole in the road, the snails looked at each other and smiled. This was the second near miss they had had in one morning, and they were both feeling a little drained but amazed by what they had overcome. With a cheeky grin on his face Bruce said, 'Ern, I'm so glad you're alive – I thought I'd lost ya!' He paused, trying to hide the emotion in his voice, and thought about how grateful he was to have found such a good friend. 'Anyway, it's a good job I found this milk carton,' he said, changing the subject. 'It makes a mighty megaphone.'

Ernie looked at the carton and remembered the first time he'd met Bruce at the compost heap, and a fantastic idea came to him. It was so good that it sent his tentacles into a spin. As they whizzed around on his head, he turned to his friend. 'Bruce, you came here for an adventure, right?'

'That's right,' Bruce replied, unsure where this was leading.

'And I know you're feeling fearless. Am I right?' continued Ernie.

'Well, umm, I guess,' Bruce mumbled hesitantly.

'Good. I thought so.' Now it was Ernie who felt like the brave one. Bruce wondered if all that 'play' with the kittens had made his friend turn a little strange. 'Cos I have a plan that will need us both to be braver than ever, and slightly "bananas", as you put it,' he said, smiling at Bruce. 'Are you up for it, my friend?' he added enthusiastically.

Bruce wondered what he had to lose. After all, they had already come so far: they had survived rapids, surfed on the back of a turtle, ridden on the legs of a wild dog, been almost crushed under the wheel of a rubbish truck and narrowly escaped becoming kitten food. 'OK, what is it?'

Ernie took a deep breath and began to explain. 'You see those cats – the mum and two kittens?'

'Yes!' said Bruce, wondering how he could not have seen them, as they had spent the last ten minutes trying to escape from them.

'Well, it's obvious that they haven't eaten for ages,' continued Ernie, his tentacles now disco dancing from side to side and his eyes almost popping out of his head with excitement. 'If we can convince them not to eat us but instead to carry us through the village while we sit on their backs, then using your milk carton megaphone we can call all the snails of Vinuella and tell them to follow us to the Olive Garden. In exchange we can lead the cats to the compost heap where they'll never go hungry again.' Ernie took a breath as he finished his long speech, and stood there beaming, waiting for Bruce to respond.

There were a few seconds' silence, then Bruce's eyes lit up. 'Awesome! That's a bonzer plan, mate. It's completely bonkers! But I love it! Let's go for it!' Ernie was just about to climb out of the pothole when Bruce hesitated. 'Only one problem,' he said. 'I know I'm big, being Aussie and all, but how do you suggest we get this great, hulking milk carton out of this pothole? It's got to be at least ten times our size!'

The snails stopped. Ernie hadn't thought of that. Suddenly his amazing, 'best ever' plan didn't seem quite so good. 'I guess we can't – it's impossible. And without the carton we can't call the other snails. All this will have been for nothing,' he said, and slumped back inside his shell, his tentacles drooping down to the floor.

Bruce looked at Ernie in disbelief. 'I don't understand how you can give up so easily. There's always another way.' So they sat and pondered.

While they were deep in thought, a car whizzed over their heads. It took them both by surprise and the force of it swept them high into the air. A few seconds later they plummeted back down, landing side by side at the edge of the road.

'Far out Ern! What in the world just happened?'

Ernie was about to reply when something fell from the sky and crashed down on top of them, almost squashing them by the roadside. Nervously, they peeked out from beneath their shells and looked at the heavy object that was balancing on top of them. To their joy they discovered that it was the milk carton. Perplexed and totally amazed, they looked at each other and shouted, 'Perfect! Let's go!' Carefully lifting themselves up they began marching forward, with the milk carton balanced on their backs, towards the rubbish bin where the cats were purring as they slept.

The plan takes shape

Half an hour had passed by the time they reached the bin and the cat family. It wasn't easy carrying such a heavy load on top of their shells and it had really slowed them down. They gently lowered the milk carton to the ground near the kittens and quietly slid inside it.

'Cat family, we come in peace!' boomed Ernie's voice. The kittens immediately looked around to see where it was coming from. 'We know you're hungry and we want to help you.' The mother cat awoke from her sleep and her fur instantly stood on end as she hissed loudly. Bravely, Ernie continued as she began stalking towards the carton. 'We know a place where there is so much food that you and your kittens will never go hungry. Every day there is fresh food and you can feast in peace.' He thought it best not to mention the dogs at this point; they would have to work that one out later. 'We will take you there if you will help us.' Ernie looked at Bruce, their hearts racing. They hoped Ernie had said enough to avoid them becoming dinner.

By now the kittens were prowling around the milk carton. One of them began to roll it on its side. 'But first, you must tell your kittens to leave us alone, if you know what's good for you,' Ernie called as he and Bruce tumbled around inside.

The mother cat made a loud meow and the kittens quickly ran back to her side. 'What do you want me to do for you?' she said, her voice soft and gentle, nothing like the snails had expected. Ernie told her the full story, and of their plan to save the snails of Vinuella village. She listened with interest.

'What are your names?' asked Ernie.

'I am Estella,' said the mother, 'and my kittens are Porscha and Rose.'

Estella was a clever cat who had learnt to survive on her own since being cruelly abandoned by her owners. However, she was not on her own any more: she now had two hungry mouths to feed. Something in her heart told her to trust the snails' curious offer. 'We will help you. If what you are saying is true, and you can take us to this place of endless food, then we will do anything,' she said. 'But we need to move fast. People come every night looking for stray cats, to take them away to a bad place.'

Ernie felt sympathy for the cats and was glad he could help them. 'Great!' he shouted. Then he and Bruce popped their heads out from the carton and introduced themselves. Ernie thought to himself just how beautiful they were. He wondered why cats had such a bad name in the snail world.

It was siesta time and everywhere was quiet as people slept in their houses. However, the village would soon be awake, and hundreds of people would be out and about in their cars. 'There's no time to lose,' purred Estella. 'Soon it will not be safe for us.'

'Yes you're right. And the snails won't hear our calls once this village comes alive with traffic,' added Ernie. Bruce rolled his eyes. He was really enjoying this adventure. It was great fun, but secretly he thought Ernie's mission to save the snails was a little far-fetched. The part he liked, though, was riding the cats down the hill and going back to the Olive Garden. But Ernie was a very good friend, the best he had ever had, so he decided to stick by him.

Estella briefed her two kittens on their mission and told them to behave. Then she carefully picked up Bruce and put him on Rose's back and Ernie onto Porscha's back. Ernie nestled himself into Porscha's soft ginger fur. Then Estella lifted the milk carton up onto Porscha's back next to Ernie and he climbed inside. The five of them were then ready to set off down the hill.

Cat food

There was an eerie
silence, like the calm
before a storm. The
summer heat had been
building over the last
few days but now the
smell of rain filled the
air. As Estella carefully
guided her kittens, the
group felt the first drops
of rain splash upon their
heads. The cats might
not like getting wet, but
there was no turning

back. Quietly Estella and the kittens tiptoed down the winding
road through the village. She knew that there were many cats
around and each of them would defend their territory at all
costs, so she had to make sure that none of them spotted her
and her family.

Once they came nearer to the snail houses, Ernie tested his
megaphone. 'Testing, testing, one, two, three!'

'Sounds good. Go for it, Ern!' encouraged Bruce.

Ernie began calling to his fellow snails. 'Snails of Vinuella,
we have found snail paradise,' he shouted with courage.
'Come with us and enjoy a new life of abundance, peace and
happiness,' he continued, feeling a little uncomfortable and
wondering if he had said enough for them to want to follow.

'That's it, keep going,' said Bruce.

'Meet us at the park just after sunset and we will take you
there,' Ernie went on.

As the rain grew heavier, they continued down the hill through the small village in the mountains, calling to the snails.

Faithfully, the two now soggy kittens trotted along behind their mother, until they all reached the park as the day began to fade.

'Phew! We made it,' meowed Estella as her kittens joined her to sit on the steps of the park. The snails slid off their backs on to the wet floor.

'Well done!' said Ernie to the cats. 'You did really well. I'm sure they must have heard us.'

Just at that moment there came a rustling from the bushes behind them. Everyone froze. The snails couldn't bear any more surprises.

'So what do we have here?' came a sly, sinister voice. Shivers ran down their backs. Ernie felt his tentacles stand on end as he wondered what danger they would have to confront this time. Bravely, they all turned around to face whoever or whatever it was that had approached them, and there standing in the half-light was a slender, jet black tomcat.

'Mmm, snails. My favourite delicacy,' he purred. 'There's not much meat on them but they taste gooood.' Bruce and Ernie looked at the cat in horror. Estella and her kittens quickly huddled together to shelter the snails.

'You'll have to get past us first,' shouted Porscha bravely.

'Is that right?' said the black cat. 'I like a challenge.'

Ernie realised that the sun had almost set and soon the other snails would be making their way to meet them in the park, and he didn't want them to end up as a gourmet delicacy for some stray cat. The black cat leapt towards them, his sharp claws out ready to attack.

'RUN!' shouted Estella.

Bruce looked around and spotted a large, empty tunnel opening in the wall. 'Over there!' he shouted, and began sliding as fast as he could towards it.

The kittens bounded on ahead. From inside the tunnel they called out to the snails, 'Quick! Faster! You can do it!' Bruce and Ernie used every bit of speed they had to zip across the ground. They slooched and slooped across the wet surface, moving faster than they had ever done before. At last they reached the tunnel and turned to see Estella desperately fighting for her family against the powerful black cat.

Ernie's Papa, Manuel, had been in the kitchen washing up when he heard a voice that sounded a lot like his grandson Ernie's. He hadn't seen him for weeks and was really missing him. He was very fond of Ernie and loved his strong sense of adventure and the chats they used to have about the Olive Garden. But one day Ernie had just vanished. Manuel was sure he had left home to find the Olive Garden. Secretly he hoped he had made it, and imagined that Ernie was having a great time there, but now he was sure that he could hear his voice outside in the street.

Quickly he went out of the house and could just about make out the three cats walking slowly down the hill where Ernie's voice seemed to be coming from. Manuel slid down the hill after them in the water gutter – something he used to do when he was Ernie's age. As he drew nearer, to his delight and surprise, he could just see Ernie sitting inside a milk carton on top of a fluffy ginger kitten. Although he thought it was a little strange, he couldn't help smiling with pride at the courage of his precious grandson. Manuel watched as the group stopped at the bottom of the hill. He was just about to call out to him when he saw the black cat approaching, and he watched the fight begin with horror. Anxiously, he watched as his grandson slid, at full snail speed, to the safety of a nearby tunnel that the gutter led into.

Excitedly, Manuel raced along the gutter, slid down the rest of the hill and whooshed straight into the tunnel where Ernie was. 'Ernie!' he said, full of pride as he swept in and knocked Bruce off balance.

'Papa! What are you doing here?' The two snails wrapped tentacles around each other's shells, so pleased to see each other.

'I heard your voice and I knew it was you,' answered Manuel. 'What is this all about, Ernie?'

As quickly as he could, Ernie explained the whole story and finished by telling Papa about his plan to rescue the other snails. 'Papa, I don't want any more snails to be taken. We have to get everyone out of here; this village is not safe.'

Manuel looked at his grandson and agreed. He trusted him and was ready to help. 'But what about Estella?' said Ernie, feeling concerned for her safety. Nervously, the three snails and two kittens peered out of the tunnel to see what was happening. Everyone held their breath and prepared themselves for the worst.

The moving floor

Estella was putting up a good fight. She was taking many knocks from the stronger cat, but despite being very tired and weak she bravely stood her ground. Once again she braced herself as the large, black tom hurtled towards her. 'Estella, watch out!' shouted Ernie, his voice amplified by the long tunnel. But it was too late. The tomcat crashed into her, and like a rag doll she found herself falling backwards and tumbling down the park's hard steps.

'Ernie, you'll have to go on without me – I can't hold him back much longer,' Estella said feebly as the black cat descended the steps menacingly towards her.

Bruce looked at Ernie, 'It's time to go!' he said.

Without waiting for an answer, he slid speedily onto Rose's back and ordered her to head for the compost heap. 'Bruce, STOP!' shouted Ernie, as loudly as his small green, snail lungs would let him. 'We need to wait for the other snails to arrive,' he said, upset that no one else had remembered them. 'If we leave the park now, they'll never find us.'

Bruce asked Rose to stop for a moment. He took a deep breath and prepared himself to tell his good friend what he had suspected all along: that his plan could never work. But at that moment, something on the village road caught his eye. He looked up and gasped. 'Far out!' he yelled. 'The streets are alive!'

Ernie looked at him, 'What, Bruce? I don't understand what you're on about.'

'Look! Over there!' Bruce pointed towards the village. Everyone stopped and looked up at the road. What they saw took their breath away: thousands of snails were making their way at speed down the wet hill towards the park.

The black cat stood over Estella and prepared to take another swipe. But suddenly he froze; he had spotted something moving in the darkness. He looked up towards the village and saw that the street had come alive and seemed to be rushing towards him. Terrified, his fur stood on end and he let out a loud hiss. Then he bounded off into the bushes with his tail between his legs.

It was a truly amazing sight: thousands of snails were surfing their way along the wet ground in the evening rain, gaining speed as they went. 'Quick, Ernie!' said Bruce. 'Tell them to come this way – if they go to the park they'll be eaten.'

Ernie dived out of the tunnel and slid inside the milk carton. 'Welcome snails. You have done well to make it this far. We congratulate you,' he said.

'Get on with it, Ern. I can hear more cats coming,' said Bruce impatiently.

'I know you must be tired and hungry but we have lots of food—' Ernie began.

'This way, snails! Over here. Follow these kittens!' interrupted Manuel, who had joined him inside the carton. Ernie looked at his Papa and smiled. Then he pulled out the yo-yo from his rucksack and attached the string to the end of Rose's long tail.

'Papa, now I know where I got my sense of adventure from,' he grinned. 'Are you feeling daring?' He pointed to the yo-yo and watched his Papa's eyes light up.

Without hesitation, Manuel slid onto the wooden yo-yo. Estella, scratched and bruised, gently picked Ernie up in her mouth and put him safely onto Porscha's back. 'OK, my friends, let's go!' he said, and the group bounded across the road, down the ramp and on to the compost heap by the river.

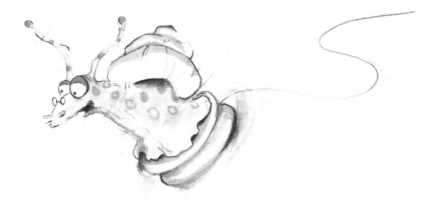

Manuel followed on the yo-yo, whizzing from side to side with a huge smile on his face. Proudly he called to his fellow snails, 'This way. Follow my grandson, Ernie!' And the large, dark mass of moving snails followed him to the safety of the compost heap.

A feast

As soon as Estella reached the compost heap she dived amongst the heaps of food in delight. Porscha and Rose skipped along behind her and leapt onto the huge pile of vegetable scraps. Ernie and Bruce slid off their backs and turned to look up the road in anticipation, watching as the snails made their way on to the compost heap. There was such a buzz of excitement as everyone began tucking into the food that lay before them. The cats and snails had never had such a feast.

When Estella finished eating, she turned to Bruce and Ernie and kissed them on their tiny shells. 'I am so grateful to you both for trusting us, and for keeping your word that you would bring us here. How can we ever repay you?' asked Estella, purring with happiness.

'It was nothing really. We couldn't have done it without you,' replied Ernie.

'Just promise us that you'll take care of this place,' added Bruce.

'That'll be easy – we love it here. This will be our new home,' said Estella.

Bruce and Ernie watched as the three cats ran off and found somewhere to settle down for the night, after their long and eventful day.

'You did good you know, Ern,' said Bruce.

'No, *we* did good,' replied Ernie.

Bruce just shrugged. 'Yeah, whatever! Anyway, never mind all that fluffy stuff. We've still got some hard yakka ahead of us.'

The two snails smiled at each other and turned to face their next challenge. The clouds had cleared and it had stopped raining, and in the moonlight they could see in front of them more than a thousand beady eyes, all looking at them expectantly. Eagerly, Ernie scanned the sea of faces. It had been weeks since he had seen his family, and to his surprise he was feeling excited at the thought of seeing them again. He had changed since he left home, and especially since he had left the Olive Garden on his mission to save the snails of Vinuella. He had grown stronger, and suddenly what they thought of him didn't matter any more. He had achieved his dream and now all he wanted was to share it with them.

Just then, he caught sight of his Papa, who appeared to be doing a demonstration of his daring yo-yo surfing to a group of snails gathered around him. Ernie looked closer, squinting his boggly eyes, and to his delight he saw that it was his family.

With joy he slid across the scraps to meet them. His family swept him up in their tentacles and hugged him. They were all so happy to see him. 'We missed you so much,' said his brothers.

'Your mama hasn't stopped worrying since you left,' said his Dad. Ernie felt loved and realised that he had been very silly to think that they wouldn't have noticed that he had gone away.

'It was unbearable to think that we'd lost you. What were you thinking?' said his mama, as she hugged him so tightly he thought he would pop.

'Ernie, please tell us what this is all about. We want to know why you've called us all here,' said his Dad. Ernie looked back at Bruce, who was standing on top of the milk carton at the front of the group, looking slightly unnerved as every single snail was looking at him for an explanation.

The black monster

Ernie slid back to join his friend. Together they slid inside the carton and Ernie explained the whole situation to the crowd, telling them how he had set out to find the Olive Garden and to prove to everyone in the village that his ancestors were right and it did really exist. Then he told about his awful ordeal when he was held captive as a pet, and that he had found hundreds of empty shells behind the fridge. As soon as he said this everyone gasped.

'So it *is* true. I knew it was,' shouted someone from the crowd.

'Yes! I heard people keep loads of us at a time and fatten us up. Then, when we are nice and plump, they cook us with garlic and eat us – as a delicacy!' shrieked another voice. Panic was setting in amongst the group and everyone began shouting.

'Let's get out of here!' came one voice.

'It's not safe,' called another. 'If we're caught we're sure to be eaten.'

The mass of frightened snails all surged forward towards the ramp.

'Don't go, please! I brought you here so I can lead you to a safe place. You have to trust me!' yelled Ernie as loudly as he could, grabbing on to Bruce just as they were knocked out of the carton by the rushing snail crowd.

'Why should we believe you, Ernie Gonzales? Everyone has always known you're a dreamer,' someone called out. The group continued forward and Bruce and Ernie tumbled around as hundreds of snails slid past.

Frantically, Manuel looked for his grandson, but he couldn't see him anywhere. He clambered up onto the top of the carton to get a better view. Suddenly there was a splashing from the river and Manuel spotted something moving in the bright, moonlit water. His heart began to pound with fright as a large, black object emerged with sea grass hanging from its nostrils. Some snails from the crowd spotted it and screamed. Manuel slid back in fright as the black monster towered above him. At that moment he heard something buzzing around his head and he began to lose his balance.

'Hola! Have you seen Ernie, my courageous slug adventurer friend? You look a lot like him, just little squishier,' buzzed the fly. 'Oh! My little amigo did good. I am his inspiration, you know. He did this because of me. I knew him when he nothing but small wobbly pet,' he said boastfully. Just then the fly seemed to sense something behind him. 'Ahh!' he yelled in panic. 'This the black river monster of Vinuella. You fight him,' said the fly. 'Fight! Fight! Fight!' At that moment, the huge monster took a big swipe in the direction of Manuel, missing his ear by millimetres but sending the fly plummeting towards the river. 'Oh no! Here I go, I can't swim!' he buzzed.

'Hola, mi amigo!' said José as he looked down at the tiny, wrinkly old snail on the carton. 'I don't suppose you have seen my two good friends, Bruce and Ernie?'

Manuel was speechless for a second. Then, once he had caught his breath, he told José what had happened and that the two friends were now lost in the crowd. José took a deep breath and roared. 'STOP!' Instantly, all the snails stopped in their tracks and looked around at the Black Monster. 'Don't go. I am not going to hurt you,' he said in a strong, soft voice. 'Ernie is my amigo, and everything he is telling you is true.' Everyone gasped. 'I have never known a creature more noble, faithful and trustworthy than Ernie. He is not a foolish dreamer but a wise, determined snail. He followed his heart and overcame great trials to discover this wonderful paradise place. He could have kept it all to himself but he wants to share it with you so you can all be safe and happy.' Everyone listened in silence. 'And now we have lost him. Has anyone seen him? He may be squashed – and his trusted, brave companion Bruce?'

'We are here!' mumbled the pair as they clambered up from under the other snails. 'But I've lost my rucksack and my hat,' said Ernie.

'Don't worry about that now. We'll find them later,' said Manuel. 'Let's just get these snails back to safety.' Bruce spoke through the megaphone and before long before every snail was safely back on the compost heap. There was a hum of excitement as a thousand or more snails talked of the Olive Garden.

Ernie turned to Bruce. 'We'll head off in the morning,' he said. 'Until then, let's get some shut-eye.' They all settled down for a night's rest, so they would be ready for a new day of adventures.

A new day

When morning came, it was an incredible sight: the floor was covered with lots of tiny sleeping snails, and in the middle were three cats cuddled together, enjoying the best rest they had had in ages. Ernie lay awake for a minute and thought about it all. Never in his wildest dreams had he imagined that his adventure would change so many lives. He wondered if this was the real reason why he had felt so determined all his life to get to the Olive Garden. Ernie was satisfied and ready to face the day's challenge: getting these snails there.

'RISE AND SHINE!' echoed a familiar voice through the milk carton. 'We have work to do,' Bruce shouted, as hundreds of small heads emerged sleepily out of their tiny shells.

Ernie looked at his friend with pride. 'Bruce, you really are the best and most fearless friend any snail adventurer could ask for,' he said.

'I wouldn't have missed it for the world, cobber,' replied Bruce. 'But there's no time for mushy stuff; we haven't finished yet. So what's the plan?' He stared expectantly at Ernie. 'You do have a plan, don't ya?'

Ernie looked up and shook his head. 'Oh Ern, you are bonkers! But let's not worry about that now,' Bruce said, laughing to himself and wondering why he had even bothered to ask.

'Something will come to mind. It always does!' said Ernie confidently.

'Yeah, she'll be apples!' Bruce said, looking at his friend as he rolled his eyes.

Once everyone was awake and ready, Ernie prepared to brief them on the next step of the journey. Quietly he hoped that an idea would come to him quickly – very quickly, in fact – as he knew that the dogs would soon be arriving for their breakfast. As he watched the snails tucking into a hearty feast of cabbage and avocado scraps, he looked over at the river. He noticed that it looked slightly different from the night before: it was now full of large wet stones that were glittering in the sun. But the strange thing was that each one looked exactly the same.

'Are you thinking what I'm thinking?' said Bruce as he slid over to join him.

'Oh yes!' said Ernie with excitement.

The snails gazed at the stones in anticipation and eventually, as they had suspected, the stones began to move. 'That's it! Let me get in the milk carton, Bruce,' Ernie said. 'Good morning José! Have you been there all night?' Ernie's voice boomed. About 50 heads popped out of the river.

'Which one is he?' whispered Bruce.

'I have no idea,' answered Ernie in a hushed voice. Then one of the turtles came up out of the river and ambled towards them. It was José.

'I thought you may need some help today so I brought a few amigos along with me,' he said.

There was a commotion as thousands of snails began to panic and retreat inside their shells. 'Don't be afraid. This is our turtle friend, José, remember?' Ernie announced with excitement.

'Buenos dias, amigos!' shouted José, munching on a few greens and laughing as he scanned the thousands of slimy snails eating their breakfast. 'Ha! I was right. It looks like you will need more than just my help.' And with that he whistled loudly in the direction of the river. 'Fellow turtles, I have some good friends here who need your help! I need you to carry some snails safely to the Olive Garden.' Instantly all of the turtles obeyed and began moving towards the river bank.

Ernie was a little overwhelmed. 'What now Bruce? How are we going to do this? There are so many of them.' He heard a loud noise coming from the road – it was barking. 'Those dogs will be here any minute!' he said.

Instinctively, Bruce slid inside the megaphone and shouted, 'Right snails, we're going to be taking a bit of a ride. This way, hop on board, and get ready for the journey of a lifetime.'

By now many of the snails had noticed the dogs so they didn't need telling twice. Hurriedly, they started moving towards the river's edge and the turtles. Ernie was still looking a little overwhelmed but Bruce seemed to have it all under control. He called out to the snails to get into groups and then slide together onto the turtles' backs.

'Looks like we'll have to make a few journeys,' said Ernie, as he looked at the thousands of snails waiting for their turn.

'Yeah! Sure thing, Ern. I'll go with the first group, so I can make sure everyone arrives safely and welcome them to the garden,' said Bruce .

'OK, that's a brilliant idea,' replied Ernie. 'But what about the dogs?' he said, as he looked back at the road.

'I'll leave that with you, my friend. You'll know what to do.'

Once the first convoy was on board, Bruce announced to everyone that they must stick on with all their strength and not let go – no matter what! Bruce, Ernie and José all looked at the snails. Although they were excited about the daring mission, they also felt slightly nervous. Each turtle had a variety of different snails on its back: young ones, old ones, strong ones and weak ones, and they just hoped that they would all make it through the rapids without losing anybody.

Deep down, Ernie knew that Bruce secretly loved the thought of going through the rapids again and leading the group, and it was great to see his friend taking charge. 'José and I will stay here until the last snail has boarded, and then I will travel with him to join you.'

Bruce jumped on to the front turtle. He waved his tentacles as a signal that they were ready – and off they went down the river, braving the dangerous rapids to reach their new home.

A friend for life

It was a huge mission, and Ernie and José delighted in it. First they had to find a way to keep the remaining snails safe from the dogs while they waited for their rides. Ernie thought quickly as usual and arranged for everyone to hide in their groups under cabbage leaves. It was a perfect plan and the dogs didn't come anywhere near them. The sun was just setting when they finally sent the last group on their way to the garden, and the sky was alight with a deep golden glow.

'Thank you so much, José, for what you have done for us,' Ernie said, feeling proud of their teamwork.

'It's easy! Not only do we turtles love to help but we also love to swim, so for us, carrying you up or down the river is great fun,' said José, beaming. 'It brings us such joy to help others. It will be good to see the Olive Garden being used and loved for the paradise that it truly is,' he added. 'We will carry you along the river any time you wish – just call!'

Ernie smiled; he somehow knew that his adventuring days were not over.

As José walked into the water and beckoned for Ernie to climb on his back, Ernie looked back at his cat friends who were resting after another satisfying feast. 'José, there is one problem. We helped these good cats to get here but I'm worried about the dogs that visit the compost heap every day,' he said. 'They managed somehow today, but what about the future?'

Jose looked at him and smiled. 'There is no need to worry about that.' As he spoke he looked up to the ramp that led to the road. 'Tomorrow they are putting up a high fence, so from now on this compost heap will be nicely protected.' Ernie looked over at the cats and smiled. He was happy to have been able to help them. Quickly he said goodbye to them and promised that he would see them very soon, and told them that if they ever needed anything to just call for José. Then he jumped on his turtle friend's back and they set sail downriver.

Cruising the rapids on the back of this amazing creature was even better than Ernie had remembered. Furiously, the water rocked them from side to side and they narrowly missed rocks and sticks. José really was a first-class swimmer. 'I could get used to these kinds of action-filled adventures,' Ernie thought.

Finally they arrived at his beloved Olive Garden. It was an amazing sight: everywhere snails were enjoying exploring their new home, and there was no one who wasn't smiling. It seemed that it had taken them no time at all to settle in and to bring this beautiful garden to life. Ernie looked around and saw that groups of snails were enjoying a leisurely sail across the pool, while others were lazing under the lemon trees and sipping bee's honey. At Lemon Harbour, talented snail chefs were cooking up gourmet recipes as the restaurant overflowed with guests waiting to sample their treats.

Then in a clearing amongst the trees he noticed a large group of snails standing in a line. As he looked closer he saw Bruce fitting each snail with a cherry pip army hat. 'Hey, Bruce, what're you doing?' shouted Ernie, as he slid over to join him.

'G'day, mate!' shouted Bruce.

As Ernie slid nearer to his friend he noticed that his hat was still on his head and he chuckled to himself. 'How in the world did you manage to keep that hat of yours on your head for this whole time?'

Suddenly Bruce seemed a little defensive. 'This hat isn't coming off my head for anyone or anything,' he said sternly. 'We all need them to keep us safe. Let me find another one for you, Ern.' And he began rummaging on the floor.

'But Bruce, you don't need it any more. We're all safe now. Plus, it isn't the hat that makes you so brave and strong. It's you, my friend. You're strong without it. It's in here,' he said, as he touched his chest where his heart was. 'Bruce, do you realise we did this as a team? There's no way I could have done all of this without you,' Ernie said, feeling a little emotional. 'Who could have led those snails through those rapids so courageously? I certainly couldn't have.'

Bruce smiled. His friend was right: he had done it. 'You're fair dinkum, Ern – a real mate.' And with that, he pulled off his army hat and threw it into the bushes.

Ernie looked around for his family. He spotted them amongst a pile of leaves. They were all cheering as Papa was teaching Ernie's youngest sister how to leaf surf. His Mama spotted Ernie and smiled the biggest smile he had ever seen. Seeing his family happy brought him more joy than he could ever have dreamt of. He thought about everything he had been through to bring them to safety and decided that it had all been worth it. Now this garden really was his paradise.

'It's only paradise if you can share it with the people you love,' he said to himself quietly.

'That's right, Ernie,' said José, who had crept up behind him and made him jump. 'Who says snails are slow?!' he chuckled.

'That's right, cobber!' said Ernie.

'What did you say?' asked José.

'Never mind. Ask Bruce next time you see him,' Ernie replied, and then slid over to join the others.

Ernie Gonzales makes it big

It has been a whole month since Ernie and the snails of Vinuella made their daring journey to the Olive Garden, and life for the snails is better than they have ever dreamed it could be. News has spread in the village, and many other animals want to know how such a small snail could have been so brave. Many have been inspired by his determination to continue believing in his dreams, despite so many challenges. So the wonderful and slightly mad fly, Captain Pablo, decided to write a story about Ernie for the Vinuella bugs' newspaper *Bugs News*.

C. Pablo: I here today with Mr Ernie (speedy) Gonzales, to find out how and why he did the crazy, I mean wonderful, thing to bring all the slugs of Vinuella to this new place. I have some questions here for you. I will just read them, OK? You just answer, OK? Good! Tell me, Ernie, why did you do this? You crazy slug!

Ernie: Snail. I am a snail.

C. Pablo: What did you say? I can't hear you. My ears a little small.

Ernie: Never mind.

C. Pablo: What or who inspired you to set out on such a stupid – I mean amazing – journey?

Ernie: Well, Pablo, to be honest, there are two reasons. Firstly, I was inspired by my Papa and his dream to find the Olive Garden and by his sense of adventure. And secondly, I wanted to make a better life for myself and to live in paradise.

C. Pablo: OK, that is very nice, Ern. Can I call you Ern?

Ernie: Errr, yeah OK, Pab!

C. Pablo: Now, Ern, many crazy people have dreams, but not all of us brave enough, or slimy enough, to follow them. How did you find the courage to start your dream, and what would you say to other special dreaming people? Hey, I like these questions, Ern. I wish I thought of them.

Ernie: Well, Pab, courage isn't an easy thing to find, but if you truly believe that your dreams will come true, then somehow you will find the courage to take the first step. I would tell other dreamers, a dream will always remain a dream if you don't take the first step and start walking in the direction of your dreams.

C. Pablo: OK, I tell them when I see them. Now my next question: we all have wobbly moments at times. I often flying into windows or car windscreens. It normal, but, my little amigo, what did you do to keep that green heart strong when you felt wobbly, especially in your belly, and to carry on sliding towards your dream?

Ernie: Ooh, that's a hard one, Pab, very impressive...

C. Pablo: Well, thanks, Ern. I have been reading papers and practising...

Ernie: There were quite a few times when things became tough...

C. Pablo: Yes, yes, tell me all, my squidgy slug...

Ernie: Like when I got stuck inside an avocado inside the fridge – that was pretty hairy.

C. Pablo: Mushy – don't you mean mushy?

Ernie: Yeah, whatever... And when I found out I was a pet. Oh, thanks for your help there, by the way...

C. Pablo: Oh, it was nothing. It was pretty good of me, though. Hey – I think I am the real hero.

Ernie: Anyway… and when I was tempted away from my dream by luscious, green olives, for a while I nearly lost it. But something in me kept believing, especially when I thought of my Papa and that I must do it for him. His words kept me strong: 'You can do this, Ernie, don't give up.' And also good friends. We can't do anything alone; we always need the help of others in some way.

C. Pablo: So it seems you are hero now, Ern. You make it look so easy. Was it?

Ernie: No, never. It was the hardest thing I have ever done, but I don't regret a single moment of it.

C. Pablo: What was the hardest part?

Ernie: Umm, that's a hard one. It was all tough. It's a bit like swimming upstream, when the water wants to pull you back, but you just have to keep swimming. I think the hardest part was deciding to leave the Olive Garden and return to get the other snails, knowing that there was a chance Bruce wouldn't come with me. I had to promise myself I would go even if I had to go alone. That took the most courage.

C. Pablo: Oh, you are nice slug friend, very mushy.

Ernie: Oh, and trying to swat you with my tentacles, that was pretty hard. You really do get in the way.

C. Pablo: Er, moving on, Ern. So what made you want to rescue the snails of Vinuella, when you could eat all the olives for yourself in the garden? You realise restaurants have closed now because of lack of snails on menu?

Ernie: I will ignore that, Pab, my old friend. Umm! That's easy – they needed my help. What more is there to say? If someone needs help, you help them, right? Nothing more complicated than that.

C. Pablo: Crazy, I mean, wise, words from a very splodgy and green Ernie Gonzales. Thanks you Ernie, and enjoy your paradise. This is Pablo Buzilo reporting from sunny Olive Garden.

C. Pablo: Can I come with you, Ern? I good at flying.

Ern: No, Pab, we are fine, thanks. We don't need any flies at the moment, but if there is an opening I will call you.

C. Pablo: I can sing: do do do do.

Ern: No, please don't. We are fine, really. I must be going.

C. Pablo: I can collect cows' dung. You must need that – it's good for house building.

Ern: Really, I must go, Pab. It's been great. Bye.

If you have been **inspired** by Ernie's dreams and his courage and you would like to find out more or to share your dreams with the author, then go to:

www.bethshepherd.com

Glossary

Aussie slang
Bananas – crazy, deranged, wildly enthusiastic
Billabong – small lake, particularly one next to a river
Bonkers – crazy, mad
Bonzer! – fantastic!
Cobber – friend, mate
Fair dinkum – genuine, honest, fair and square
Far out! – great, good – or bad!
Good on ya – good for you, well done
Hard yakka – hard work
Ripper – great, fantastic
She'll be apples! – it'll be all right!

Spanish terms
Amigo(s) – friend(s)
De nada! – you're welcome
Encantado! – I am pleased to meet you
Hasta luego – see you later
Hola amigo – hello friend
Hola, buenos dias – hello, good morning
Me llamo José – my name is José

I would like to thank a number of people, without whom my dream of telling Ernie's story would never have been realised. Manoj, from Instant Apostle, for giving me the opportunity to publish this book and believing in my vision from the start; Nigel, for his wisdom and input in drawing out the best from Ernie; and Lisa, for bringing this book to life with such wonderful illustrations, and bringing pictures to my words.

First published in Great Britain in 2012

Instant Apostle
The Hub
3-5 Rickmansworth Road
Watford
Herts
WD18 OGX

Copyright © Beth Shepherd (text), Lisa Buckridge (illustrations) 2012

All rights reserved. No portion of this book may be reproduced or transmitted in any form or by any means, electronic or mechanical, including photocopying, recording, or by any information storage and retrieval system, without permission in writing from the publisher.

British Library Cataloguing-in-Publication Data

A catalogue record for this book is available from the British Library

This book and all other Instant Apostle books are available from Instant Apostle:

Website: www.instantapostle.com
E-mail: info@instantapostle.com

ISBN 978-0-9559135-7-0

Printed in Great Britain